Review Copy

The Bellboy

The Pillboy

The Bellboy

By

Anees Salim

www.hhousebooks.com

Paperback ISBN: 978-1-910688-67-0

Cover design by Jo Dalton

Typeset by Jennifer Case

Published in the UK

Holland House Books
Holland House
47 Greenham Road
Newbury, Berkshire RG14 7HY
United Kingdom

www.hhousebooks.com

To
Adah Anees, Omar Anees and Shameena Anees

1

As they would go to a holy city to die, people came to Paradise Lodge to end their lives. Young and old. Men and women. Able-bodied and ailing. Like migratory birds, they arrived from places Latif had never heard of. It was as if it was the closest point to the after world, as close to heaven as the weatherworn jetty that stood to the back of the lodge, across a narrow, slimy, canal.

From the top of the highway, Latif had his first glimpse of the lodge; a tallish building that had not seen a lick of paint in years, and wore a sombre brown, akin to the sepia of holy cities. The huge bay window on the fifth floor had a few missing panes and looked like a gaping mouth with the front teeth knocked out. As he walked nervously down the highway, Latif thought the lodge had the appearance of a demented old man, smiling blankly at a younger clump of architecture.

Over time, Latif had started to suspect that people checked into the rundown, short-staffed lodge only to die. Some survived, changing their minds at the last moment, probably daunted by fear or guilt, or even by the advertisement for an upcoming lottery that drifted in through an open window. Some simply succumbed. A fat ledger, made fatter by the dogeared pages, sat on the counter in the lobby, a pen suspended from a twine glued to its spine. Latif would kill time turning its yellowing leaves, reading the entries as solemnly as one read headstones. His eyes would linger over the names against which the checkout details were not recorded. Blurry red lines ran vertically across the pages, creating columns, and under the one titled *Purpose of Visit*, guests wrote either *Business* or *Personal*, never *To Die*. Tracing the dead guests' handwriting, usually a shaky scrawl or, occasionally, a surprising copperplate, he often wondered how they had bid farewell to their families before leaving home for the last time, and if their hands had shaken when they wrote in the ledger.

When the people on his island asked after his job in the town Latif pretended to love it, but he secretly thought of the lodge as a house of death and decay. His first day at work had left him shattered, opinionated. He had carried a freshly laundered bedsheet down a gloomy corridor to Room No. 117 and spent a long time knocking on the door. He then reported the unresponsive guest to the manager who clicked his tongue and collected a bunch of keys from the drawer. The manager was a stout middle-aged man who never ceased to remind Latif of a savage-looking Mexican footballer he had seen on a neighbour's TV. As they walked down the corridor, he wondered if he should tell the manager that he had a doppelganger in Mexico, who played on pitches that looked like pastel green carpets. But it was his first day at work and he did not know if the manager liked football enough to be flattered by such a comparison. And the manager had the angry eyes of one who did not welcome conversations, so he decided to follow him in silence, imagining them to be two tough wardens proceeding to an even tougher inmate's cell, the keys jingling in sync with his superior's laboured gait.

The manager hammered on the door for a few minutes, then chose a key from the bunch and slipped it into the hole. Latif didn't expect the door to open, but it did, and he hid himself behind the manager, anticipating something bad, and then gathered enough courage to peek into the dingy little room. The guest hung from the ceiling, his face flushed with an almost comical look, suggesting there was no dark side to death, that death was just another laughing matter. Latif immediately wanted to walk away from the lodge, never to return. But the thought of his dead father's photograph on the living room wall, of the lunch his mother had packed for him, and the library-like silence of his insular village held him there.

The manager strode into the room, skirting the pool of urine that had collected on the floor beneath the dead man, and opened the cupboard in the corner. Latif remained in the corridor and looked past the hanging guest at a window that framed the branches of a gulmohar tree—full of flowers, full of birds, full of life. The manager picked up a folded sheet of paper from the middle rack and read it cursorily. Then he put it back and anchored it with a ballpoint pen. Next, he picked up a wallet and opened it. Latif, new to the job and even newer to the scenario of a suicide, watched uncertainly as the manager extracted a few currencies from the wallet and pushed them into his shirt pocket. He turned his head away and glanced towards the jetty and watched the afternoon boat pull away. Had he caught it, he would have been home in less than an hour, lying on the narrow bed in his bare little room that afforded a distant view of the olive waterbody through a coconut grove. The next boat was due in an hour, and he knew he would not take it either. No, he would catch the one that departed just before daybreak and take the early morning boat back to work a day later, every second day. That was the arrangement with the lodge. However much he wanted to quit, his father's photograph on the wall and the lunch his mother cooked for him in the small hours would keep him tethered to the lodge.

The manager locked the room and walked back to the lobby, and Latif trailed him nervously. Barely into the third hour of his first job, he had already witnessed a dead man being looted. Abruptly, he felt grown-up. An eyewitness to oddities. A keeper of secrets. Until a month ago, his mother had worked in a small factory that sat at the edge of the island, next to the pier, shelling cashews. She smelt of woodsmoke and cashew apples, even after she left the job. Handling smouldering cashew shells all day had left her fingers spongy, their skin scarred and smelly, rough-like sandpaper. When she could no longer hold the club that cracked cashews open, she left the job reluctantly. It was from the owner of Quilon Cashews that she heard about the vacancy at the lodge. More than the money it brought, what appealed to her about the job was the small chance of Latif getting lost in the mainland. A boat ride to the town, a leap over the canal, and he was at work. A boat ride to the island, a ten-minute walk from the pier, and he was home. If the boat capsized, he could swim either to his workplace or home, depending on where the vessel sank. He was a good swimmer. Everyone on the island was.

The manager dropped the keys into the drawer, smoked a cigarette and only then did he pick up the phone to report Room No. 117 to the authorities. Latif expected the police to arrive as soon as the phone was dropped to the cradle, the sirens of the police jeep and the ambulance overlapping onto one another. The police took hours to come. The ambulance would not arrive till late afternoon. The drive under the gulmohar was a red carpet by then, speckled with the yellow of anthers, and the police jeep came to a halt just short of the floral setting.

'The guest is not responding,' the manager told the police.

'Didn't you try to open the door?' a policeman asked.

'No, we were waiting for you to come.'

Latif followed the policemen and the manager down the corridor, careful not to tread on the shadows of the capped heads. He no longer thought of himself as a jail warden and the dead man as a feral inmate. He was numb in a way he had never been, not even when he heard of his father's death, he found himself completely empty of thoughts, grief and imagination. The manager chose the wrong key from the bunch and tried to open the door. He chose three more wrong keys before using the right one. When the door fell open the manager recoiled theatrically, his mouth half open in feigned shock. Latif remembered the Mexican footballer being tripped to the ground and rolling on the pitch in fake pain, soliciting a penalty kick. A new detail caught his eye; the front of the dead man's trousers was wet, and his big toes dribbled to the floor, as slowly as a hospital drip. The room now smelt strongly of urine.

A policeman picked up the suicide note from the cupboard and read it in a patch of sunlight while his colleague dragged a chair to the window and started to write on a clipboard. He gave the dead body long, occasional, glances, as if drawing inspiration from the deceased to write a story. Latif did not wait for the rest of the proceedings. Hurrying down the corridor, he grabbed the lunch his mother had cooked for him in the light of a sooty 40-watt bulb, using a spoon to save the torments that the condiments gave her permanently bruised fingers. He sat down on a bench in the lobby and opened the oily paper parcel. Then he ran out, the lunch in his hands, and made himself sick under the star fruit tree at the back of the lodge.

2

*A*mong the loosely strung archipelago, his island was the farthest from the town and the biggest of the six. Where the river met the land there started the legend of Manto Island. The bust of Manto, a fat man with a handlebar moustache and a double chin, sat on a pedestal near the pier, facing the river, discoloured and defaced. Though the bust was the colour of tar, Latif knew Manto was white, that he served as an administrator to the archipelago during the colonial period. Though the sculptor had squeezed a half-smile onto Manto's thick lips, Latif doubted if the administrator had ever smiled at the natives until he had to take a boat out of the archipelago and then a ship out of the newly-born India. Every time he passed the bust, Latif wondered what had qualified Manto to be immortalised in granite, and what folly had he committed that his bust be vandalised with flint and grease. The island no longer paid any attention to the statue, even birds had stopped sitting on its head and smearing it with their droppings. And when Latif saw it on the neighbour's TV his heart leapt, and when he spotted many villagers on the screen—uncles, cousins, neighbours, the young tailor who stitched his clothes and the old barber who cut his hair— he wanted to call them out by their names. But, in spite of the islanders smiling shyly at the camera, the report spelled doom for Manto Island.

If the ecologists were to be believed, Manto Island was slowly disappearing, being gnawed away by high tides. But Latif never believed the ecologists, and to prove them wrong he kept a tab on the margins of his village and found the dimensions unchanged; the land had not shrunken even by an inch, the river had not grown any wider. The island appeared robust enough to outlive his generation, unless it had secret plans to collapse from the middle and let itself be sucked to the bottom of the river.

Everyone who lived on the island thought it was immeasurably big, and in that false sense of enormity Latif's house was a long distance from Manto Road, a gruelling ten-minute walk from the pier. He lived on the other side of the island, near the marshes, at the end of an alley padded with fallen leaves and fenced by an unbroken line of quickstick plants.

Hardly a mile away from his home, the pier sat at the north end of the island: a hurriedly constructed finger of concrete that jutted out into the river like a bridge abandoned halfway through construction. A shed stood a few feet away, propped up on four pillars furiously scrawled with charcoal sketches of genitalia. The teabag-like testicles and the angry curls of pubic hair always ran a wave of suppressed laughter through Latif. A footpath worn smooth by generations of islanders going to the mainland to work, trade and philander – only to return home sombre-faced – twisted through a wooded estate and joined the street that, despite the fury unleashed on the statue, still bore the name of Manto. He had considered Manto Road to be the busiest place on earth until the day his school went on an excursion to a city, south of the archipelago, to visit a museum of archaeology. The city was so big and busy it burst the bubble of Manto Road forthwith, and Latif started to think of the urban side of his island as a mere rotogravure that belonged to the very museum he was visiting. It took him months to look again at the street with some amount of respect, and still then he did not stop lusting after the lives of the boys who lived in apartments so tall he imagined their windows to shut against moving clouds.

The night before his first day at work, Latif's home hardly slept. His sisters took turns to iron his best clothes until their pleats turned blade-like while he, cooped up in his room, carefully employed an eyebrow pencil to darken the hint of a moustache into something that resembled a flattened centipede. By the time he went to bed, the kitchen light had already come on and his mother had started to cook lunch for him while the rest of the island was not yet contemplating breakfast.

It was still dark when he left home, escorted by his mother and sisters up to the little wooden gate. His footwear made short squeaks on the slushy alley floor and, once he turned the corner and fell out of his family's eyeshot, it was the only sound that assured him that he was not wandering in a dream. In the empty alley he felt like a shadow without a body, one-dimensional and weightless, invisible even to the dogs that guarded the houses along the way. Roughly an hour later, he felt even more invisible as he stood in front of the collapsible door of Paradise Lodge and rapped on it apologetically for attention.

A stout man, whom he seemed to have known back from Manto Island, stared sleepily at him for several minutes through the grille before unchaining the door and letting him into a spacious lobby, lit by a single lightbulb. Latif placed a hand on his heart as if complaining of angina and mumbled his wish to meet the manager. The man plopped onto a chair and placed a little board on the countertop which read *Manager*. 'Where have I seen him?' Latif thought. His heart sank when he noticed a saffron thread on the manager's left wrist; it somehow suggested that no matter how doggedly he worked, he would be constantly frowned upon.

'Yes?', the manager grunted.

In a lowered voice, Latif introduced himself as the candidate sent by the owner of Quilon Cashews. He expected the expression on the manager's face to melt into consideration, or even kindness, but the manager merely pointed to a bench and asked him to wait. As he sat down, his back turned to an arched window, he suddenly remembered where he had met the manager, or rather why he had looked so intensely familiar. He looked like a Mexican footballer who, to judge from the yellow and red cards he kept earning, was not a nice person to know.

As the light hardened on the windows, he surveyed his new workplace with curious eyes. The false ceiling, the wooden panelling, the shape of the windows and the ornamental lampshades suggested that it had once been a premium boarding house, when the bellboys were probably liveried, and the watchmen worked in shifts. But now the walls were streaked with dirt, the furniture looked like antique pieces on sale and the ceiling fans had yellowing blades and squealed like trapped mice. Behind the counter was a single window that framed a star fruit tree. As he sat staring through the window, the tree silently dropped a fruit. He felt a boyish urge to run to the tree, pick it up and sink his teeth into the flesh the colour of Brazilian jersey. It was too early for something as sour as a star fruit, but poor sleep had turned him hungry and he felt guilty about opening the lunch pack when it was not even properly morning. His empty stomach burning with hunger, he sat still and watched the lobby limp to life.

The other bellboy was an old man who walked slowly around the lobby as if bogged down by elephantiasis, though his legs were thinner than Latif's. Latif watched the old man fill frosted plastic jugs at the water dispenser and arrange them on a tray, open a cloth bundle and take bedsheets out, run a wet rag over the countertop and dust the fat ledger. Watching the old man was a rushed apprenticeship in housekeeping for Latif. He was to later do what the old man did now.

At the stroke of seven, a middle-aged lady walked into the lobby and, mistaking Latif for a lodger waiting to be checked in, smiled politely at him. The manager looked at the clock which, more than telling the time, hinted at the heyday of the lodge. Just when Latif thought he was about to compliment the lady for her punctuality, the manager started to shout at her for being late by half an hour. Anger made the manager look more like the footballer, and Latif took the shouting as his formal introduction to the lady; her name was Stella, her job was to sweep the front yard and mop the rooms, and she lived just three streets away. Stella paid little heed to the manager, so Latif knew this happened every morning. She went to the anteroom, and when she returned she was wearing a faded shirt over her clothes and wielding a long-handled broom. She opened the fat ledger from the backside where it doubled up as the muster roll and scrawled her signature on it, then dragged the broom past him.

'Stella, this is the boy I was talking to you about yesterday.' The calmness in the manager's voice surprised Latif, 'He will do full day shifts on alternate days. He will sleep on the bench. When you have done with sweeping, tell him what he is supposed to do.'

Stella smiled at him again. Her smile was no longer polite, if anything it was sympathetic. She went out to work her broom on the forecourt until she could gather a heap big enough to make a decent bonfire out of.

Half an hour later, Latif opened the ledger from the backside and carefully drew his signature between two blue lines. It was about an hour after he was absorbed into the rusty mechanism of the lodge that Latif found himself holding a bedsheet in one hand and knocking courteously on the door of Room No. 117, waiting for a dead guest to respond.

3

*H*e had taken them for siblings—the fair, fleshy lady for the elder sister and the dark, well-built man for the devoted younger brother, a good decade between them. But the trip to the drugstore with the scrap of paper the man had thrust into his hands proved him wrong. The druggist frowned at the chit and said he did not have condoms in banana flavour and glanced towards a dispenser that offered only two variants: strawberry and bubble gum. Latif, having never tasted a strawberry in his life, settled on the latter. Walking back to the lodge shame-faced, he was certain that the old druggist and his assistant would be laughing at him and discussing how audacious of a boy (he still looked boyish in spite of having turned seventeen six months ago) to have asked for a pack of condoms, unless it was for his father, in which case how irrational of a father to have sent a boy to pick up rubbers. The possibility of his father being wrongly accused of such thoughtlessness saddened and angered Latif.

The way the islanders had stopped seeing Manto's bust, Latif had long ceased to notice his father's photograph on the living room wall. Taken not long before he drowned in the river he had lived all his life by, it was not the ideal picture to be put up in remembrance; he was neither smiling nor keeping a straight face, not even looking directly at the camera but squinting at the ecologist who had been posted in the village to assess its longevity. The ecologist was a tall, bony man who, in his first week on the island, was repeatedly mistaken for the new priest at the seminary, because no one from the mainland stayed for long on the island. He seemed to be on an eternal walking tour, collecting muddy samples in beakers, staking sticks into the slushy borders of the island, picking up stones, and drawing patterns on ancient trees with a blue chalk. On a late afternoon, on his way to the marshes, he stopped by Latif's home and said a hearty hello to his father, who was tilling the front garden to plant cassava. Latif's father turned ecstatic about the intervention; he knew every nook and corner of the island, every mood of the river, every yard of the archipelago, and he talked to the ecologist like a homegrown professor through an interpreter. A recorder sat on the parapet, listening, while the ecologist clicked pictures of every interesting object around. This included Latif's father, who, owing only to the shape of his moustache, was nicknamed Mandrake. Before the ecologist and the interpreter proceeded to the marshes and Latif's father went back to tilling, they all agreed to meet at the pier the next week for a trip down the river to one of the neighbouring islands. Long after they were gone, Latif could not stop marvelling at the skill of the interpreter, his effortless ability to bridge two languages with just his voice. As the sun dipped through the coconut grove and made the olive river a splash of orange, he aspired to be an interpreter. The next morning, though, he switched back to his ambition to be a sailor, onboard a ship that cruised from port to port, continent to continent. Never did he want to be a bellboy, running ridiculous errands like this.

The dark man opened the door at the first knock and received the pack of condoms without a smile, without questioning Latif's choice of flavour, and refused to take the money left from the errand. Latif's first tip. Since he had started working at the lodge a month ago, he had lingered on many doorways and smiled his best smile after showing the guests to rooms, lugging their luggage up the stairs when the old lift malfunctioned, bringing them extra pillows, fetching them sodas, and wishing them awkward good nights. All that he got in return was a cursory smile and a reminder to close the door behind him. He slipped the money into his pocket and glanced past the man. The lady was nowhere in evidence. But he heard her in the bathroom, water crashing over her plump body.

Back in the lobby, he lay down on the bench and imagined the dark man sitting on the edge of the bed, waiting for the lady to emerge from the bathroom, wrapped in the white, frayed towel that the lodge provided along with crisp white bedsheets and two sample size soaps. As soon as the manager started snoring behind the counter, Latif's hand went in search of his penis, and as he stroked it into the size of his forefinger, both in length and width, he saw the lady dropping the towel and lying down. Her inside was like the cross-section of an onion, pink flesh curling layer upon layer. Elbowing the dark man away, Latif climbed onto the bed and sank into the mount of her flesh. Her cheeks smelt of neem soap, her hair of perfumed oil and her crotch the way his own armpits did, a sharp tang that was not entirely unpleasant. He cleared his throat to cloak the encouraging grunts that the shaky bench occasionally gave, and forced a long fit of coughing when he came and his penis coiled back to the size of his thumb. Like his first tip, this was something new, his first orgasm outside the four bare walls of his little room. He would forget neither.

Rattling like a beggar's bowl, the collapsible door woke him. A bunch of shapes stood in the dark, like refugees seeking shelter. Latif went behind the counter to wake the manager, who smiled at him for a moment, then stared coldly. When the light came on, they saw five men—three standing in a huddle under the awning, two beneath the gulmohar tree. The three were policemen in civvies, their boots and body language said as much. Two of them came into the lobby when the manager rolled the door back, and one placed a photograph on the counter.

'Is this person staying here?' asked the policeman, tapping on the photograph.

Latif edged closer to the counter so that he could have a good look at the photo. He saw a couple standing against a one-dimensional pine forest fringed with paper pansies and plastic aloe vera. The posture and the setting suggested it was the mandatory post-wedding photograph people used to go to studios for until a few years ago. The man stood stiff, one hand thrown over the lady's shoulder, the other placed on her left sleeve; the lady stood at an angle, her body half-turned towards her husband, smiling at the camera. Though she was much younger and leaner in the photograph, Latif recognized her without an effort; he had been right on top of her a few hours ago, moving like a rocking horse.

The manager opened the ledger and started to leaf through it, mumbling that his shift had started only in the evening and that he didn't know who had checked in before that. Latif wanted to intervene and say that no lady had shown up since the previous night, even when he knew he could not bring himself to lie to the police, but he felt inexplicably protective of the occupants of Room No. 209. He willed to slink away and take the clanking lift to the second floor and facilitate their escape, leading them down the footpath that ran from the side of the water tank past the star fruit tree to the gap in the backwall. From there they could whisk themselves away to someplace safe.

The manager's finger stopped at an entry in the ledger, and he announced that only one lady had checked in since the afternoon and that she was accompanied by a man. The men waiting under the gulmohar were beckoned to the lobby. Latif instantly identified one of them as the husband in the photograph. What time had done to him was in sharp contrast with what it had done to his wife; he had grown thin, turned darker, lost most of his hair and, as if in compensation, acquired a beard. A flower from the gulmohar had landed on his shoulder, and it looked like a floral print on his otherwise plain shirt. The policeman pushed the ledger towards him and touched the page with a corner of the photograph. The husband shook his head in confirmation, then he brushed the flower off his shoulder.

'Show us the room,' commanded the policeman, and the manager nodded at Latif.

The cables groaned overhead as the lift moved reluctantly up the shaft and shuddered to a halt on the second floor. Latif rolled the grille back to release the two policemen and the husband into the dark corridor; the others, probably discouraged by the notice that restricted the number of passengers to four, had preferred to stay downstairs.

The knocks on the door were met with muffled footsteps that came close to the door and then retreated hurriedly, and it was a long time before the dark man opened the door. Latif expected him to shudder and back off at the sight of the lady's husband, but it was the husband who winced and dropped his head. He kept his eyes fixed on the floor until one of the policemen put a hand on his elbow and led him gently into the room, leaving Latif alone in the corridor. From where he stood, Latif had a view of the crumpled bed, two pillows propped up against the headboard and the cupboard in the corner. The lady, like the last time, was nowhere to be seen, and Latif thought she was in the shower, oblivious of the men in the room, probably working up lather on her breasts. Then he heard her sob, standing out of his view, and the men turned their heads towards the source of the quiet lamentation.

Latif did not know whether he was expected to stay or leave. He preferred to linger; everyone loved a soap without commercial breaks. Moving a few steps backwards, he blended into a shadow and leaned against a pillar and waited for the characters to settle into their places and begin the opening scene of this dark romantic dramedy.

The husband sank to the edge of the bed and put his

elbows on his knees and cradled his face on his clenched fists. When he began to talk, Latif was disappointed by the flatness of his voice, the complete lack of theatrical flourish in it. It was not late, he said. Latif wondered if he was referring to the time of the night. It was not too late, he repeated, the children had been told their mother was visiting her parents, her parents had been told she was with a friend, the neighbours had been told she was on a pilgrimage. Nobody knew yet that she had run away with their children's English tutor. At the mention of his specialisation, the English tutor touched his nape and craned his head to look at the ceiling. The wife stopped sobbing, and Latif heard her snuffle. He willed her to step into his line of vision and speak up, to tell her husband that she had slept with the tutor, to open the cupboard and bring out the pack of bubble gum flavoured condoms as evidence of the infidelity. But she said nothing, she had even stopped snuffling.

Latif waited for the drama to move on, to escalate into an argument and then into a fistfight. All of a sudden, a deep gurgling sound filled the room, and it was a long moment before he realized that the baton of grief had been passed on to the husband. He had opened his clenched fists and veiled his face with his long fingers. Every time he watched football on the neighbour's TV, he backed the trailing team but turned neutral the moment the scores were levelled. He had a such soft spot for losers and sufferers. Watching the weeping man, Latif quickly shifted his loyalty to him.

The English tutor had turned his gaze to the ceiling again and crossed his hands so defiantly across his chest that Latif wished the policemen interfered and ordered him to arrange his hands in a more respectful way. The weeping man moved Latif almost to tears, and he wanted to bring him a glass of water. The wife's silence angered him, he regretted running an errand for them and plotting to help them sneak out through the gap in the backwall. He should not have taken sides without considering both sides of the story. The policemen watched the crying man patiently, probably they didn't know what to say, probably they knew it was best for him to vent his hurt this way. But he stopped sobbing abruptly and, after drying his eyes with a balled-up kerchief, stared out of the door. Latif stood still, pretending to be a poster on the pillar. The man put on his reading glasses and stared harder, and spotted Latif, the solitary spectator. Springing to his feet with such ferocious energy that the English tutor quickly unfolded his hands into a defensive posture, the husband marched to the door. For a moment, Latif thought the man was going to cross the corridor and slap him for eavesdropping, but he stopped at the door and slammed it shut. The door opened again even before Latif could think of walking back to the lift, and the husband wagged a finger at him. He shuffled up to the door, bracing himself against a tight slap, but the man slipped a currency into Latif's shirt pocket and closed the door gently behind him. Latif's second tip. Until he was back in the lobby it didn't dawn on him that he had been tipped by two men who had screwed the same lady in different capacities.

The manager was fast asleep in the dark lobby, his head on the counter, the ledger for a pillow. Latif knew if he went back to sleep he was certain to miss his boat. The first boat almost always left the jetty on time, nearly empty on its way to the island, overcrowded on the return trip, crammed with islanders who, like him, made a living out of the town's small needs. The second boat would not ply until midmorning, by that time his mother would be sick with worry and would have made several oblations to the local mosque for his safe return, even a trip to Quilon Cashews where she would beg the owner to call the lodge and ask after him. By the time the second boat pulled in, the whole of Manto Island would know he had missed the first one. For fear of dozing off, he sat on the steps and watched the tips of cigarettes glow under the gulmohar. The night looked on the verge of ending, birds had already started to tweet.

Not long after the clock struck five, he heard the lift going up and, a short while later, rattling its way down, ending its journey with a heavy metallic thud. Men passed him, then the woman, and cigarettes were thrown to the ground and stamped out under invisible feet. It surprised him how quickly and peacefully everything seemed to have ended. He wondered if the husband and the English tutor had shaken hands in the end, or even exchanged shirts the way footballers did before leaving the pitch after a cup-tie. He could not decide who was the winner and who was the loser, and without that knowledge he didn't know whose side he should be on.

Just as the darkness began to lift, the English tutor came to the lobby to return the key, laden with a suitcase and a rucksack. He looked immensely relieved - he was almost smiling.

Latif ran to the jetty.

4

*T*he long queue went around the ticket booth and, stretching past Quilon Cashews, ended on the edge of the road where Manto's bust sat facing the river, his nose dripping with dew. Though the sun would not be up for another half an hour, the river already reflected the tall trees that grew along the bank, and Latif thought of them as the ghosts of the recently drowned islanders, lined up to watch the morning boat arrive. He had his lunch tucked under his armpit, the oily stains on the paper parcel spreading to the armhole like a deep sweat mark.

The man who stood in front of Latif shook a cigarette out of a crumpled pack and fished out a box of matches from his trouser pocket. A sense of pride filled Latif when he saw his sister's name on the matchbox, written in a thick stippled font inside an ornamental border that turned to crescents at the corners. It was deeply endearing to know that Beema Matches were in circulation long after his father had died.

Latif was fourteen when his father turned his sisters' bedroom into a matchbox factory. As a direct consequence of this, the girls had to shift their books, boxes of trinkets and beddings to his room. The sudden loss of privacy upset him, but what let him completely down was the name of the new venture; his father had decided to name it after his youngest daughter instead of his eldest son. His father's former businesses—dry fish, mango pickles and bicycle repairing—had also borne his sisters' names before they went bust. Hurt to the core, he faced the river and shed silent tears, and prayed for the matchbox factory to go up in flames. But the day his father brought home bundles of matchbox labels from the town Latif forgave him. Fresh from the press, the labels smelled of glue and glowed in sunlight. They looked so expensive Latif feared no one was going to buy Beema Matches. He stole a fat bundle and hoarded it and bartered the labels in daydreams for fast cars and cruise ships. The name on the label occasionally pained him, and the day the first box of matches came off the assembly line, which consisted of nothing more than his father's long sinewy hands, Latif spoke his mind out, tears streaming down his bony cheeks. In a rare show of affection, his father wrapped a hand around his shoulder and promised to call his next undertaking, most probably coir manufacturing, by the boy's name. The prospect of another business petrified Latif's mother, though she held her tongue in the best interest of her weeping son. *Latif Coir Works*. The fluidity of the name rang in his head for days. But his father died six months later, and the girls moved their goods and chattels back to the orphaned matchbox factory.

His father's death had made headlines, not because he drowned, but because the ecologist he was travelling with also did. The canoe had sunk near an uninhabited islet hardly a mile north of Manto Island, and his father could have swum to safety and waited for a boat to pass by, but he floated around in search of the ecologist who, coming up for air, caught hold of his leg and dragged him to the bottom of the river. Only the interpreter survived to tell the tale in different languages to television cameras.

In the days that followed his father's burial, Latif tried to imagine the ecologist's family in vain. He seemed to have come from nowhere and his body appeared to have been carted away to a place where no one mourned him. Latif had stopped envisioning the ecologist's final resting place when, about a month later, his widow made her appearance. She sat in an open boat and dropped flowers into the river where the wind had tipped the canoe over. She had short hair the colour of contrails, and the villagers sized her up with mild distaste because she wore three things no woman in the village had ever dared to: a sleeveless blouse, a pair of sunglasses, and short hair. Unmindful of the deep frowns, she carried a handful of marigolds to Latif's home and requested to meet his mother. But his mother would not give audience to strangers until forty days had passed since his father's burial, which made Latif, on the threshold of sixteen, the temporary head of the family. The lady expressed her wish to shower the flowers on his father's photograph. But the house had none. She requested them to hang one where everyone could see him and remember his sacrifice; such a hero should not go unsung. When she raised a hand to push the sunglasses to her scalp, Latif noticed her armpit, clean and powdered. From the moment she had been spotted in his front yard, he thought of her as someone perpetually irate, and his opinion didn't change even after she had heaped praises on his dead father. Neither he nor his sisters understood a single word she said until the interpreter translated the condolences and eulogies in the tone of a documentary film. Shy to be translated, Latif didn't utter a word in return. From her handbag, she extracted a brown envelope, evidently containing money, and tried to press it into Latif's hands. Before he could take it, the interpreter intervened, declining the reward with a crisp shake of his head. Not wanting to belittle the bereaved family, the lady quickly returned the envelope to the bag. Latif's heart sank; how inaccurately the interpreter had construed his family's state of affairs and how readily she had complied. They left soon afterwards. On their way out, the lady stopped by the oblong patch of earth his father had raked a few days before his death to plant cassava stumps. Mistaking it for his grave, she showered the marigolds onto the bed of coffee-brown earth and, joining her palms under her chin, observed a minute of silence. The interpreter stroked his beard to hide his smile. Latif wanted to tell her his father had been laid to rest behind the mosque, at the end of a ribbon of red earth that ran through thorny bushes. But he was somewhat certain that the interpreter would swallow the translation to save the lady such an embarrassment in the first month of her widowhood.

The ghostly shadows on the river lengthened as the sky began to lighten above the trees. Latif heard the horn of the morning boat from somewhere beyond the next island. The long queue undulated as if it stood in the path of a hurricane, and then went nearly still as if the turbulence had passed. With the changing velocity of the wind, the soft throbs of the engine drifted in and out of the pier. A long time after the blare of the horn reached the island, *Jesus* came around the bend, an orange mass of wood with broad green stripes on its sides, swathed in grey mist. The nearer the boat came, the more restive the waiting line became, and the moment the hull brushed against the flank of the concrete finger the queue disintegrated into a mob and gushed into the vessel. Gripping the lunch pack with both hands, Latif climbed in through a window and secured a seat in the first row behind the driver's cabin. That was his box seat to the boat's navigating system, it afforded him a good view of the driver as he took *Jesus* down the yawning archipelago. Above the steering wheel was an open rack, stacked with sun-bleached lifebuoys, and every time Latif looked at them he thought of wreath bases awaiting flowers.

The boat was crowded but quiet; it was too early for pleasantries and political talks. People preferred to doze off, dreaming their private dreams, shuddering in their incoherent little nightmares. Latif spent the forty-minute trip to the town wide awake, either attempting to read the faces of sleeping commuters or watching the houses on the nearer bank, imagining the arrangement of furniture behind the almost identical exteriors. He could never read faces beyond the age, nor could he imagine anything beyond the front doors. Though he didn't sleep a wink, he clamped his eyes shut the moment the tallest coconut tree in the whole archipelago slid into view. It twisted almost like a paperclip halfway up the trunk and leaned out of the islet like a detail escaped from a horror movie. The tree was the cue for him to fake a sleep from which he would not wake until he was sure that the islet had fallen out of sight. Somewhere near that islet his father had been dragged deep into the river by the man he was trying to save.

From the boat the town looked broken and littered. Every morning the same picture of desolation welcomed him—blanched backsides of buildings that had more presentable facades, growing hills of garbage that occasionally took the shape of a Christmas tree and a rusting dredger whose dereliction was almost completely hidden under thick hanks of morning glory. The jetty was the butt of the town, as dirty, as smelly. He disembarked without hurry and picked his slow way across the canal and down the footpath. Where the path curved like a horseshoe, he slipped in through the gap in the backwall.

Stella was already at work, dragging her long broom on the carpet of flowers under the gulmohar. He liked Stella, a kind woman who was roughly his mother's age, though he never liked what she did to fallen flowers every morning, scraping them into a little red mound and setting them on fire with a sprinkle of kerosene. The day they became friends he wanted to express his displeasure over the floral bonfires she made. But fearing that she might see only a joke in his concern, or see nothing more than a boy's eagerness to sound poetically mature, he confided in her instead, narrating in a conspiratorial tone what he had witnessed on his first day at work. She hushed him up, and made him swear on his mother that he would not talk to anybody about the manager stealing from the dead man, not even to his mother.

Every second day, a sense of achievement filled Latif as he opened the fat ledger from the backside and signed on the muster roll. He did it with his own pen, which heightened this feeling, and made him believe he was doing a white-collar job. But once he closed the ledger and put it next to the little board that read *Manager*, he found himself completely bereft of any sense of pride. He followed the routine of filling the frosted plastic jars with cold water from the dispenser and taking them up on the rattling lift, to knock on doors and wait like a milkman. Then he carried a pile of bedsheets on his forearms like a young maid and made beds in rooms that were waiting for guests with an air of emptiness. At the stroke of one, he took the lunch pack to the shed near the water tank. Stella was already there, straddling one end of a bench with her lunchbox open between her knees. Latif straddled the other end – they looked like overgrown children occupying a seesaw. Chewing with varying degrees of force and indulgence, they swayed in and out of conversations. Stella always talked about her family, mostly about the way her husband drank himself silly, and Latif about his village, mostly about its oddball characters, some of whom he had made up in his head for reasons he didn't know himself. His favourite character was a boy of his age and build, carefully moulded with the vigour of Tarzan and the virtues of a school-going Lincoln. His name was Ibrahim, Ibru for short. Bullies behaved themselves in his vicinity and every girl on the island swooned at the sight of him, Latif's sisters excluded. He was not sure if Stella liked Ibru's adventures and acts of charity, but she listened intently, without questions, with a knowing smile.

Crafting a lunchtime story in his head, he gave Stella

half a fried fish. She gave him half a boiled egg. 'Ibru caught this fish,' he said as she brought the piece to her lips. But before he could explain how Ibru had caught it—diving into the river and staying underwater for so long that everyone started to fear for his safety, and then coming up with a pearl spot fighting for its life in his hand—the manager appeared behind the water tank and beckoned him to work. A guest urgently needed a taxi.

'Let him finish his lunch,' Stella protested.

'He can finish the lunch after finding the taxi,' the manager said impatiently and walked back to the lobby.

Only when he was rinsing his hands under the tap did he remember the fallacy of the story he was about to tell Stella. The fish he claimed to have been caught by Ibru was neither big nor pearl spot. It was a fair-sized climbing perch, with the sad, drooping eyes of his sisters. As he walked to the taxi rank, he decided to compose his stories more carefully in the future, to make his characters more foolproof.

5

*H*e heard *Jesus* blare in the distance, coming in with the afternoon passengers. It was his day off; on such days he imagined the lodge non-functional, the town non-existent. Without his presence and involvement he was unable to picture any place to exist, except the island.

He squatted on the rim of the neighbour's coconut grove, holding his crude fishing rod out, his lips quivering with a silent plea to the fish to swim by. As on every second afternoon, he had promised his mother fish for supper, though she did not expect him to bring any. His fishing skills did not amount to anything, and he always went home with the empty little rattan basket and a coconut shell filled with unspent bait. This particular stretch of river was fast losing its biological reserves; that was what the ecologist told his father two days before they both perished in the river. He blamed it on the train of houseboats that oozed diesel onto the freshwater. But

Latif secretly blamed it only on his own clumsiness, for he regularly spotted the other islanders tread the bank with garlands of fish writhing by their sides.

He heard *Jesus* blare again, going away with the afternoon passengers.

One trick of fishing was to keep the water so still that your reflection resembled an overexposed x-ray image of your head. On the surface of the river Latif looked younger than he was. He, like his mother, was of small build while his sisters had taken after their father and were tall and well-boned, which made people mistake him for the youngest of the three. He waited for his moustache to thicken and darken, and his voice to harden. Even after much wishing and silent pleading, life refused to grant him such luxuries.

There was a slight movement at the end of the string, and he sensed the twine go taut. The bait was being nibbled. To make the reel even steadier he wrapped both his hands around the rod. He decided to count, he would yank the reel out of the river at fifty. But even before he reached twenty, the water's edge began to pleat as a houseboat skimmed around the corner. The reel went slack, and he heard the fish slither away. Not a small one, to judge from the plop it made. He agreed with the dead ecologist that houseboats were the bane of fishing. The houseboat was a big brown fish in itself, the whale of the backwaters, it scared smaller fishes away. A white man stood on the deck, looking at Latif through the viewfinder of his camera. Realizing that he had become the accidental subject of photography, he sat still, his eyes downcast, as the houseboat hummed by. The white man lowered the camera to his chin and looked at its display, and then showed Latif a thumb in approval or gratitude.

Latif steadied the reel again and waited for the next fish.

A few years ago, the island had earned considerable amount of attention because of a picture published first in an international magazine and then in all local dailies. When it appeared in the newspaper that his neighbour subscribed to, followed by the drone footages of the island on the same neighbour's TV, Latif had to strain himself to believe that it was the place he had lived all his life. The island looked only vaguely like a bra to him until he read the caption, and then he stared at the picture without blinking and the pattern emerged clearly. The two circular masses of land, connected by a narrow strip, did look like a pair of upright breasts, and the mangroves on both sides resembled green bra straps. The islanders had a long look at the picture and started pinning their houses with their fingertips. Latif's was on the right breast, on the left curve of the areola. The girls who went to the convent on the mainland came home crying, their breasts having been stared at and mocked, but the boys took pride in the aerial shot and secretly boasted that they hailed from a place where even the topography had a dirty mind.

If the shape created ripples, the news that followed sent shockwaves through the island. Manto Island was not to last forever. The girls came home from the convent crying, half-expecting the island to be already gone. The boys, too, looked worried. The day a boatful of experts docked at the pier, Latif witnessed people round them off with a look of fear and hatred, as if they were shipwrecked pirates. How long would the river take to swallow the island? The interpreter relayed the question to the ecologist who looked over his shoulder at the calm river before answering. Twenty years, he said concernedly, twenty-five at the most.

Latif wanted to laugh. Twenty years were a continent away. In twenty years, he would be elsewhere, on his own, his sisters would be married off and elsewhere, his parents, too, would be elsewhere. When he thought of his parents, his mental picture of elsewhere began at the red clay path that wound through prickly bushes and ended under a clump of cashew trees. But in those twenty years he would be mature enough to cope with the loss of his parents, and even if deaths still frightened him, his wife would be by his side to comfort him.

Twenty long years. There was no need to sell off the house to some unsuspecting soul, pack the bags, drag the sheep out of the barn, bundle the chickens into wire cages and run to the pier in time to catch *Jesus*. There was ample time to plan the exodus.

The death of the ecologist seemed to have somehow extended the island's expiry date. In the months that the island existed without the service of an ecologist, Latif occasionally went to the marshes to check if the river had started to gulp down the mangroves. And every time he walked home reassured. But then came the new ecologist, the new reminder of the doomsday. He was a much older man who, unlike his predecessor, looked unfriendly and spoke very little, leaving the interpreter almost redundant. He pedalled around the island on a rented bicycle, the interpreter tagging along on his ancient Raleigh, and leaned occasionally against coconut trees, smoking his pipe and facing the river like Manto's bust. One afternoon, Latif passed the two on his way to Quilon Cashews, carrying the lunch for his mother he had helped his sisters cook. The interpreter motioned him to stop and pointed him out to the new ecologist, mumbling a low-pitched introduction to the serious-looking man, who knitted his eyebrows as if Latif had caused some major destruction to the island's ecosystem. He said something which the interpreter did not find worthy of translation. Latif wondered why ecologists always spoke in English. The interpreter dug into his shoulder bag and brought out a brown paper parcel the size of his sister's science reader, secured with a jute string. He placed it in Latif's hands and waved him on. Standing in the veranda of Quilon Cashews, Latif and his mother undid the jute string together and peeled back the brown paper, as if they were jointly inaugurating a little enterprise of their own. It was his father's photograph. The dead ecologist had taken it two days before the canoe keeled over. He remembered the widow with shaven armpits emphasise the need for decorating the hero with a picture in the front room. *Hero*, Latif sneered inwardly. Saving a man from drowning was indeed a heroic act but dragging the saviour to death was plain cheating. The photograph brought tears to his mother's eyes, but he thought they were a bit forced, probably she shed them only because other nut shellers had come to the veranda to look at the picture. In the evening they removed an outdated calendar from the front room wall and put the photograph in its place. The girls, too, were moved to tears, and he accepted their tears as honest.

With the man of the house on the wall, the front room looked important and whole. Latif arranged his textbooks on the shelf beneath the photograph to lend his father the look of a well-read man, just in case someone thought of stopping by. None, except the man from the electricity department, did. But he didn't spare the hero so much as a glance, directing his fullest attention to the electrical meter, above which Latif's father had occasionally placed a lump of magnet to make the disk crawl.

In the first few days after the photograph had been hung on the wall, Latif felt he was stepping into somebody's house, passing through a well-furnished study. But as the days went by, his father's eyes turned accusatory, especially when his mother returned from Quilon Cashews with fingers scarred and sore. The day she started to leave a spoor of bloody fingerprints across the house, Latif volunteered to work.

A sudden heaviness gripped the reel, and the tip of the rod bent a little. He felt the string tighten, as if the hook had gone under a stone; he started to count, racing to fifty. Just as he was to flick the rod up, he heard his mother's voice filtering through the coconut grove, calling him home.

'Ibru,' she yelled, stretching his short pet name into a long angry chant. 'Ibrooo, Ibrooo.'

The line strained again, and the rod shivered. His mother's voice hadn't scared the fish away, unless it was a stone that the hook had got stuck under. With a quick twist of his arm, he hauled the rod up and a catfish tossed itself into view, dancing against the backdrop of the darkening river.

The fish landed on the grass and continued to dance, big and wheezing. A cold shiver ran up his legs and didn't stop until it reached the tip of his sweaty nose. He picked the fish up by the fin and put it in the rattan basket, and as he walked in the direction of his mother's insistent voice, a nervous excitement took hold of him. He felt he had baited a mermaid.

6

As they lunched, Stella spilled the beans: there was not a single room in the lodge that had not been forced open at least once because the guest had failed to show up in the lobby well past the check-out time. There was even a guest who died in the lift, as he was still breathing when they broke into his room. Cab drivers smiled sympathetically at the passengers they dropped off under the gulmohar, though they never had any qualms about overcharging them. They could almost always tell the intention of the passengers by their reaction to the sudden fare hike. Those who picked a fight were not meditating death, and those who paid without a word were probably too preoccupied to argue.

'You know what my husband calls this place?' Stella asked. 'Suicide Lodge.'

Suicide Lodge! Latif felt he was employed at the location of the scariest movie he had ever watched on the neighbour's TV. The castle in the movie was a far cry from the lodge, but the long corridors and the old lift now gave the appearance of having been carefully constructed to heighten the eerie air of emptiness.

Noticing the slow way Latif ate, Stella tried to underplay the mystery that shrouded the lodge. The deaths did not occur in a short span of time, she said, they happened over forty years or so, and she, being the only employee who had lasted four decades in service, had to witness them all. Not all deaths were unnatural, though. Some guests had gone to bed after setting alarms but never made it to sunrise. But the people who had chosen the lodge specifically as their place of death outnumbered those who died of natural causes. There were even a couple of them who requested wake-up calls so that their bodies would be discovered before they started to decompose. When there were deaths in the lodge, Stella usually skipped her lunch; dead guests killed her appetite and made her think of the lodge as five floors of mortuaries, topped with a misleading neon signage.

To calm his nerves, Latif thought of a schooltime story, which he remembered every time death was discussed. He did not remember the details, but the moral of the story never left him. He vividly recalled the mother who took her dead son to Gandhi (or was it Buddha?) and implored him to bring the child back to life. The lady was asked to collect a clove (or was it a mustard seed?) from a house where no one had ever died. The mother, after several rounds of the village, returned empty-handed, inconsolable. So, there was nothing sinister about someone dying in every room of a boarding house that had been in existence for over forty years. Nevertheless, Stella's secret unsettled him much the same way the parable from school had saddened him. He had remembered the dead child in the story when the news of the canoe sinking near the islet was mumbled to him by an uncle. But the moral of the story did not offer him any solace.

'Ibru caught this.' He gave Stella half of the catfish.

'Stella bought this.' She gave him the tail end of a sardine coated in a thick layer of chilli sauce.

As they ate, he wondered why Stella had told him about the deaths in every room. He had witnessed one on his first day at work, and his mother, fearing that he would never return to the lodge again, assured him that a dead body was a good omen to begin a career with. He didn't completely believe her theory, though it gave him enough confidence to take the morning boat to work.

Just to prove that he was not rattled by Paradise Lodge's reputation or by its sobriquet, he wanted to narrate the story of the mother and the dead child to Stella, but he was not sure if it was Gandhi or Buddha who used clove or mustard seed as a paradigm to underline the inevitability of death. Buddha, most probably, for Gandhi had easier ways to demonstrate truth, and mustard, clove being less common among condiments. So he withheld the parable and merely pretended to be untouched by the information. But the approaching night wrecked his forced indifference, and he dreaded walking the poorly lit corridors of the upper floors. After sunset he tried not to use the noisy lift, the stairs appeared less likely to have paranormal presence, and when he absolutely had to take the lift he kept his eyes averted from the mirror wall next to the control panel, fearful of spotting a pallid face in the mirror, a kind smile directed at him. Ghosts looked most terrifying when they were courteous, at least in movies. The same was true about doctors, they smiled most kindly when they had bad news to break. *If your fingers stay infected, and considering that you are highly diabetic, this can eventually lead to amputation.* The doctor smiled at his mother as he wound gauze around her fingers.

A week after Stella confirmed that the lodge was indeed the house of death, Latif was asked to sign above the dotted line on a voucher and handed his first salary. He accepted the money shyly, as if he was being tipped, smiling gratefully at the manager but not meeting his eye. Then he retired to the lavatory behind the lobby and hungrily counted and recounted the remuneration in the light streaming in through the slatted window. There was a long list of things he wanted to splurge his salary on; a pair of sports shoes, a T-shirt with a big heart made of red sequins, a pair of sunglasses he could wear on the boat, and a mobile phone – even though Manto Island fell far beyond the reach of the nearest transmission tower. The reality that he was not supposed to buy even the cheapest thing on his wish list angered him. He worked back-to-back shifts, smiling like a mannequin to improve his chance of being tipped, he ate only half of the lunch, saving the rest for dinner and he slept on a rough bench, and he still could not buy anything for himself. One moment he wanted to dump his family and live in the town for the rest of his life, the next he longed to get off *Jesus* and run home, waving the currencies, fashioned like a Chinese fan, in the nippy air blowing from the river.

By the evening he had counted the money so many times that he could tell the denomination of each currency with his eyes shut, and when the night fell he surprised himself by paying a quick visit to the druggist and buying a pack of condoms, ribbed and bubble gum flavoured – the rack that used to stock strawberry flavour was empty. He didn't try to guess what the old druggist and his assistant would say once he left the shop; emboldened by the salary, he no longer cared. He pushed the pack deep into his trouser pocket and walked back to the lodge like a seasoned rebel. As the night deepened, he sensed his penis distend and prod the pack, as if asking for an appointment. The night passed in a series of fantasies to the accompaniment of the manager's deep snoring.

The morning boat was unusually crowded. In the dim light of the jetty lamp, he saw the ecologist and the interpreter board *Jesus*, followed by a group of men dressed in blue T-shirts with a graphic earth on the chest. They looked like children roused from sleep and rushed out on a picnic. The Blue Shirts were laden with big black bags that clanked like sacks of nails when they were lowered to the floor. Latif smiled at the ecologist and the interpreter, expecting to be called to their side and introduced to the Blue Shirts as the son of the island's hero, but neither so much as smiled back. As the tallest building of the town disappeared from his view, he noticed that Mathan, who lived in the same alley as he, except for three months which he spent in a jail for picking a priest's pocket, was also onboard, standing suspiciously close to the ecologist and his entourage. At the prospect of the ecologist's wallet parting ways with him in the same fashion as the priest's, Latif puckered up his lips to stifle a smile that was threatening to stretch from ear to ear. Mathan bowed his head a little and smiled reverentially at the ecologist, who, innocent of the knowledge of this thin man's livelihood, returned the smile and nodded. Latif's face bloated with suppressed giggles. Craning his head out of the window, he let the wind puncture his face. He simpered at the ripples that the boat ploughed through the river, but abruptly his thought changed its course and a sudden fear gripped him. What if a pocket was picked and *Jesus* was made to dock by the police aid post that sat on the edge of the first island of the archipelago? What if everyone on board was frisked? How would he explain the pack of condoms? His heartbeats quickened when he spotted people he knew from his island, people who knew his mother. He just hoped the three months in jail had reformed Mathan and the smile of reverence that lit up his face came straight from his heart. But petrified by the undivided attention Mathan paid to the ecologist, he considered dropping the pack of condoms into the river when no one was looking. But he knew it was a bad idea, the pack was certain to float around for a while, stared at by a boatful of people.

When Manto Island appeared in the distance, he heaved a silent sigh, and the moment the flank of the boat scraped against the pier he scrambled out and hurried home in the pumpkin light of the warmthless sun. The fences along the way, made of an unbroken line of quickstick plants, had started to flower, a spit of lavender among the bottle green leaves crusted with morning dew.

His mother sat on the doorstep, feeding chickens, the girls were doing dishes by the clump of banana plants, and the sun perched an inch above the roof, nearly the colour of the rooftiles. He paused at the doorway to dig into the wrong pocket for money. His fingers touched the pack of condoms, slightly misshapen from the journey, and it stung his skin like a needle. His mother's eyes moistened when he thrust the wad of notes into her hands, and he thought there was something forced about her sadness. The girls were more forthcoming, they smiled and gave him a distant look of gratitude.

The condoms still left him jumpy. Dreading his room would be searched in his absence for any sign of squandering, he decided to keep the pack in his pocket until it could be opened and applied in peace. When his mother returned from the grocer's in the evening with the month's supplies, he announced his hair needed trimming and left for the island square.

7

Riverview Salon made a mockery of its own name, offering only a view of the fern-covered sidewall of the seminary. Latif waited for his turn on a piece of furniture that might have been a sofa once, the springs under the tattered seat relaying insignificant vibrations up his bottom every time he shifted his weight. He turned the leaves of a much-thumbed-through film magazine while the salon chair swivelled and whined under the weight of someone's idea of a perfect pompadour. He stopped at the centrespread. A plump lady with massive thighs sat on a red barstool, dressed in a pink two-piece bikini—the top piece was so tightly packed that her cleavage looked like a subway for toy cars, the lower piece resembled a chewed-up bubble gum strung across her groin in the shape of a cartoon smile. In a corner of the page a comic bomb had its short wick on fire, and above the sparkle was the name of the lady written across a series of cubes, each cube a different colour, an alphabet per cube. Bina Bomb.

He found the name as voluptuous as its bearer. Her upper thighs looked like fresh dough, the rest like freshly baked baguettes. Her lips were the sort of purple Latif's family acquired only on days his mother cooked beetroot. One of the stapler pins pierced through her navel and nearly distorted the oval. As if he was trying to rub a smudge off the glossy page, Latif worked his thumb on her crotch, demure-faced for the benefit of the busy barber. He felt an urge to take Bina Bomb home, not in her bikini, though. He would hold her hand and lead her down the alley fenced with flowering shrubs, and, to the utter disbelief of his family, declare themselves as man and wife.

'Put that down and get on the chair,' said the barber. The salon chair was empty.

Not that it mattered, but his sisters never approved of his hairstyle. He could never imagine his head without the locks that covered his earlobes with luxurious curves. The day he was allowed to go to the salon alone he had started to cultivate them, more out of the need to hide the top of his left ear, which was flat as if cleaved with a knife, than of any particular love for curls.

'Don't cut the sides,' he told the barber when the pair of scissors started to clatter close to his left ear.

'You don't have to tell me that every time,' the barber

muttered. 'You are the only one on the whole island who keeps such a hairstyle.'

Walking home, he felt very special.

When the night fell, he closed the windows which he usually left open at night for the wind from the river and latched the door that he had never fastened since his father's death. Then he plugged the keyhole with a screw of boat tickets, just in case someone turned curious about the sound of latches being dragged into loops.

He swung his legs onto the bed and eased the trousers down to his knees. At the sight of his own nakedness, his eyes turned slumberous with lust. Smiling shyly to himself, he opened the pack of condoms. There were three pouches inside, shiny pink in colour, and when he ripped one open his fingers were coated with a powdery greasiness. He made the tip of his penis kiss the ring of rubber and unrolled it carefully into a tube. It was evidently meant for something bigger, making him wonder if genitals thickened with age the way bones did. If not, his nuptial life was at serious risk, his future wife was certain to stray. Curling his fingers around the uncertain hardness, he moved the condom up and down. For some reason, he remembered the manager and the football player who looked like the manager. With an effort he tried to concentrate only on Bina Bomb, on the parts of her body that looked freshly baked. Gradually the condom became less ill-fitting, but it still hung dispiritingly slack. He had a long way to cover before achieving the perfect fit. When he fantasized kneading the lady's bosom, he almost heard the salon chair creak, and then he heard loud bangs, the door shivering under somebody's clenched fist. The door muffled the sound of his name being called, but he could still sense the urgency in the voice of his sister. He quickly pulled up the trousers and closed the zip, the condom still hanging limp on him, and then he slipped the pack of condoms into his pocket and opened the door. His mother and sisters faced him, tears streaming down their faces, and he thought all their sadness had the same kind of honesty this time.

'What?' he asked, swallowing.

'Uncle Koya has died,' his mother sobbed.

Uncle Koya was her elder brother, the man with the darkest prayer rump Latif had ever seen, who lived a few alleys away, at the tip of the left bra strap in the aerial picture of the island, where the mangroves began. Latif disliked him to the point of scratching abuses on his gate because he referred to Latif's father as a joker and always made fun of his family for the businesses they started with a fanfare and invariably ran into a wreck.

'Come,' his mother grabbed him by the wrist and dragged him out of the room. 'Let's go.'

'Let me put on a shirt first,' he protested.

His sister was already holding out a shirt to him.

In the weak light of the torch Beema held, they pushed their way down the alleys walled by flowering quickstick plants. The night had swallowed the lilac flowers, but their fragrance scented the route to Uncle Koya's house right up to its front yard. The mourners were just trickling in, mostly neighbours, women in their loose night coats, their heads covered, men in tight vests, the hair on their chests exposed.

Uncle Koya's son gave Latif a kufi cap and a copy of the Quran and instructed him to sit by the body and recite surahs until a replacement was found. Latif opened the Quran on his lap and reeled off, first in a lowered voice and then, as his stage fright wore off, in a louder and more rhythmic tone. He felt uneasy, though. The condom was as much on his conscience as on his penis, and he refused to look at Uncle Koya every time a mourner walked in and the shroud was lifted.

The river was closer to Uncle Koya's house than his own, and he heard it ebb and flow as he listened to his own voice, the only authoritative sound in the house that was now teeming with mourners. Between the surahs he caught his cousin's eye, who gestured at him to lower his voice, Latif was almost shouting the verses out, attracting unpleasant glances from the mourners. When his replacement finally arrived—a young Quran teacher from the madrasa—Latif did not feel like closing the scripture and leaving the scene. Something held him back, a strange sort of inertia, and it was the thought of the approaching sunrise that finally made him stop reciting and walk out of the house.

In the front yard, people sat in little groups on rented foldable chairs, probably evaluating Uncle Koya's life in murmurs or contributing details to his obituary. The garden had acquired a tarpaulin roof while he had been indoors, cutting off the view of the night sky. He walked down the last stretch of the alley in thinning darkness and did not stop until he reached the edge of the rugged bank. Facing the river, he undid the zip, as if he wanted to relieve himself, and with a flick of a finger unburdened himself of the wrinkled condom. Then he dug into the pocket and squashed the pack against his thigh. Pulling it out almost angrily, he tossed the pack to the high tide with a quick swing of his hand. A canoe passed in the distance, rowed by two thin silhouettes, a glimmer of yellow flickered inside the lantern that sat on the central thwart. When it crawled around the marshes, Latif walked back to the house in mourning, and halfway up the alley the hum of surahs greeted him. In the approaching morning, he was certain about being chosen to be one of the pallbearers, and the certainty of it made him feel considerably better, nearly happy.

In search of his mother, Latif wandered through the house, and finally found her behind the kitchen, making black tea for mourners in a big pot on a makeshift hearth. Her eyes were bleary, but if it was from crying for her brother or kindling a fire with her breath he could not tell.

'I am going home,' he told her. 'I will take a bath and come back in a while.'

'Why do you want to come back?'

'For the funeral. I am taking a day off.'

'No,' she whispered, looking furtively around. 'Go to work. Nobody will notice your absence.'

8

The town stayed distant and detached, refusing to befriend him even after a month had passed since he had become a bellboy. Other than a handful of people who worked at the lodge, Latif knew no one, and no one knew Latif. He had become familiar with the streets of the town, but not its ways. When he met people whom he seemed to have met before, Latif strained himself to trace them back to the island.

So, when the tall, bearded man opened the door, Latif tried to place him on the island, wanting to ask if he lived by the pier, or at the other end where the marshes were. But the man looked blankly at the bellboy before stepping aside and letting him carry the jug of water to the side-table. Then he went to a window and looked in the direction of the jetty, of which only the spike of the lightning arrester was visible above the trees.

It was one of the better rooms of the lodge, better

because of the spacious bed, the extra set of windows, the dresser next to the door, the geyser in the bathroom and the air conditioner that turned asthmatic a few minutes into running. It even had a fancy number: 555. It was one of those rooms where the moderately rich and remotely famous used to stay when Paradise Lodge had still been the pride of the town, with walls that were distempered every second year and the neon signage that blinked all night as if in mockery of the surrounding, lesser, boarding houses.

The man had checked in the previous night—when Latif had probably been reading the Quran aloud, the condom rubbing against his thighs like hardened glue. There were bags on the bed, open and empty, their contents strewn all over as if he had misplaced something precious and had been searching for it all night. Latif wanted to ask him if he was from Manto Island, but he was not supposed to ask questions to lodgers, only to answer their queries and return their smiles.

Stella laughed out loud when he said the man in Room No. 555 looked familiar. Finding that he had no lunch (his mother had been making black tea in Uncle Koya's backyard when she should have been cooking for him), Stella had asked him to help himself from her lunchbox, which he did shyly at first, in small morsels, eating like the way his sisters did when they visited relatives, and then without inhibitions, faster and in bigger portions so that he ended up consuming most of Stella's lunch.

'He looked only familiar to you?' she asked, her eyes widening in mock wonder. 'He is an actor.'

'I don't watch movies,' he said. He had once heard the son of his neighbour, who was as young as Latif but talked already like a man of great wisdom, say that with an air of self-esteem while Latif sat on the floor drooling over the Sunday movie.

'What about your friend Ibru?' she asked, smiling vaguely.

'What about my friend Ibru?' he echoed her, not understanding the question.

'He doesn't watch movies either?'

He quickly appraised Ibru's list of avocations. 'Ibru watches all the movies,' he stammered. 'He comes to the town just to watch movies.'

'Since you don't watch movies, let me tell you who this man is. He is a somewhat famous actor. But I don't think he is doing well in movies lately. Why else should he stay in a place like this?'

That was true. No one successful chose to stay at Paradise Lodge anymore. It was as dead as a cemetery, people seemed to walk in under some compulsion or other. Early in the afternoon, when the manager ended a brief intercom call and told Latif that he was wanted at Room No. 555, he was elated. He considered telling the actor that he loved his performances, though he did not remember watching any of his movies on the neighbour's TV. He thought that would make the actor happy, even make him grateful enough to make friends with him. There was a chance of them hitting it off; the actor appeared to have a long stay on his mind, he had brought a little mountain of luggage with him. But as he knocked on the door, Latif knew he was too scared to talk.

The door was open and the actor sat at the table, his head in his hands. A syringe lay at his left elbow, its barrel empty except for a few droplets, and a smouldering cigarette rested on the porcelain ashtray that bore the lodge's name - a relic of the better days.

'Are you unwell?' he asked before he could stop himself.

The actor looked at him uncertainly. 'What makes you think I am unwell?' He didn't sound angry, nor anguished.

Latif pointed at the syringe. 'The medicine,' he said.

The actor frowned at the syringe as if he had not noticed it until then. He picked up the cigarette and took the longest drag Latif had ever seen anyone take. 'Yes, I am unwell if being unhappy is an illness.'

Latif failed to understand his words. But he already

had a story to take home, to tell his mother and sisters, his sisters especially—he had seen an actor in flesh and blood, he had talked to an actor.

'Why did I call you?' the actor asked himself, tapping on the side of his head as if to activate his brain. 'Yes, I remembered. Is there a laundry service nearby?'

Latif nodded and looked towards the bed where dresses were piled in little colourful pools, as asymmetrical as the islands that he travelled past every second day, and the actor pointed at one that sat at the centre of the bed. 'Get them ironed. And ask them to be careful with the white shirt. I don't want the dirt from the iron plastered all over it.'

As he collected the dresses from the bed, he noticed a bunch of syringes partially hidden under a pillow, and he took pity on the actor for the amount of unhappiness he had to be vaccinated against. He draped the dresses over his arm, one over the other, placing the white shirt on top.

'What is your name?' asked the actor, as Latif made for the door.

'Latif,' he said proudly. That was one more detail to the story he would take to the island—an actor knew his name. 'When do you want this back?'

'As early as possible. Ask them to be careful with the white shirt. It is an expensive one.'

Latif felt a twinge of pain at the prospect of the actor packing his bags and leaving soon.

The laundry shop was a ramshackle shed that sat next to a tea stall, run by a man who dragged a heavy, charcoal-filled iron across a table like a toy locomotive. Latif sat on a milestone and watched the launderer press the actor's clothes and pile them up in a corner of the table. When it was the turn of the white shirt to be ironed, Latif rose to his feet and repeated the instructions to keep it innocent of even the littlest of dirt marks. Then he walked briskly back to the lodge with the warm clothes stacked on his forearms, reminding himself of the prim housewives he had seen in detergent commercials. The white shirt was on top of the stack, like alabaster icing on a multi-layer cake. As he passed the gulmohar the wind caressed the branches and a drizzle of flowers came down, he leaned protectively over the stack, but the windfall steered clear of him. It was in the light of the lobby that he noticed the logo embossed on the pocket of the white shirt. It looked like an ornamental U at first, but at a closer look he saw the head of an antelope woven out of white thread, its extravagant antlers almost dwarfing the head they stemmed from. It seemed to be the only shirt in the world to have such impeccable thread work on the pocket, sewed onto the chest as a token of appreciation for the actor's achievements. Latif felt happy that he was holding it in his hands, and sad that he would never own a shirt with such a personalized motif on the pocket. He had never worn a dress that had a logo on it, and he had never lusted after one until now.

He rapped on the door with his elbow and the actor opened it with a furrowed face as if he was rehearsing the role of a man roused from sleep. Latif placed the stack gingerly on the bed like they were clothes tempered out of glass. It gladdened him to see that the bed was still a mess, the actor had not started packing yet. He waited for the actor to inspect the ironed clothes, if not the whole bunch, at least the white shirt, and commend him for a job well-done. But the actor merely nodded and went to the table to light a cigarette.

'You smoke?' he asked.

'Yes,' he lied, pleased that someone had thought he was old enough to smoke. A cigarette was tossed to him. He caught it in his cupped hands but didn't know what to do with it. He was offered a light, which he declined and slipped the cigarette into his pocket. 'I will smoke it later,' he said and found himself holding a hand out. The actor looked at the extended hand for a long moment and then took it and shook it briefly, without smiling. The missing smile did not bother Latif, he felt he had already been handsomely tipped. That was another detail to the story he would carry to the island— he had touched an actor.

The warmth of the ironed clothes lingered on his forearms even after he was back in the lobby. The manager had left for the day, leaving the responsibilities to an old man Latif saw only rarely, who spoke little and slept like a log, without a sound. Latif put the cigarette in an empty pack he found in the bin under the counter and hid the pack behind the tower of old newspapers next to the water dispenser. He would smoke it another day, he would probably smoke it with the man who had donated it to him.

He could not wait for the birds in the gulmohar to start chirping and herald the dawn. The island must be waiting for him to chirp his story out.

9

*C*amp Office. The big house next to Quilon Cashews had a new ochre board hanging from its awning. It had not been there when Latif had left for work a day ago, but he had guessed someone was moving into the house that had remained shut and silent since the death of its owners, an old Anglo-Indian couple who looked like siblings; he had seen a little army of men weeding the garden, scrubbing the walls and then daubing blue paint on them. Intrigued by the board, he stopped by the gate to peer in. A bald man dressed in shorts and nothing else, whom Latif recognized as one of the Blue Shirts who had travelled to the island with the ecologist a couple of days ago, stood behind the fence, gazing through a telescope-like apparatus skewed towards the river, as if he had been appointed to keep an eye on the high tide.

The ecologist sat in the veranda, his bare feet pressed to the railing, smoking his pipe. The interpreter was nowhere to be seen. Maybe it was too early in the day for anything to be translated. He heard *Jesus* depart with a long honk, as if mocking the shirtless man for his bulging stomach.

The fences had more flowers than before, more purple and prominent. Hunger turned him into a cross country runner, and he reached home gasping for breath, ravenous. The rusting padlock hung on the front door, the front yard was not yet swept, the coop stood closed and the hens were clacking inside. After letting the hens out, he peeped in through the latticed window and found there was no sign of life inside except for his father's half-smiling photograph. His mother and sisters must have slept over at Uncle Koya's, a house that had ceiling fans and fluorescent lamps, plush sofas and a refrigerator, even a thin television that looked glued onto the wall. His mother must have stayed out of grief and decorum, and the girls for the little luxuries. He sensed hunger die down and a wave of rage tremble through his body. Nobody cared about the breadwinner who spent his nights on a narrow shaky bench, who drank cold water from the dispenser when pangs of hunger struck, who bought lottery tickets with the money he earned from running errands to the liquor store. Nobody valued his sacrifices and waited for him to come home. He wished he had not left the cigarette behind, he could have smoked it in protest, in solidarity with all the young and old who were mindlessly leeched upon.

Yells ready at his throat, he waited for his thankless family to return, resolute about not eating anything until his mother wept and the girls went down to their knees to beg. When he heard them at the gate, he ground his teeth and worked his toe on the sandy earth, drawing a swastika beneath the broken steps. At the sight of his mother carrying his breakfast on a porcelain plate covered with a banana leaf, hunger returned to him like a landslide, but his rage stayed, though considerably allayed. Balancing the plate on his knees, he started to stuff his mouth with fistfuls, pushing the wrathful words down his gullet while his mother unlocked the door, and the girls threw open the windows.

He didn't speak a word till the evening, when he went to the neighbour's house to watch television, hoping to a catch a glimpse of the actor on one of the channels. But dinosaurs were on TV, and he didn't have the courage to request the channels that played more earthly movies. He quietly occupied the place designated to him—on the floor next to an armchair, his dirty feet tucked under his thighs to avoid soiling the carpet—and watched the beasts caper about a park. For a moment he thought of telling the neighbour's wife about his encounter with the actor, but she always responded to him with grunts and occasionally offered him tea unsmilingly in a glass that, like his place on the floor, was reserved for him.

As the movie was nearing its end—the dinosaurs were

on a rampage and people were on the run—he heard his mother's voice, spread thin by the expanse of the estate, calling him home. 'Ibru. Ibrooo. Ibrooooo.' He wanted to watch the movie to the last frame, but the lady of the house flicked a stern finger in the direction of his home.

'Ibrooo. Ibrooooo. Ibrooooooo.'

His name, called out in varying timbres and modulations, worked as a beacon in the dark coconut grove as he bolted through the bumpy terrain. Gasping for air, he reached his mother and, mumbling protests, followed her into the dimly lit house.

The smell of his lunch being cooked an hour before sunrise woke him up. Rousing, he remembered he hadn't told the girls about the actor, he had been too angry to talk to them all day, and at night they had been busy doing dishes. He went to the former matchbox factory to see if they had woken up, but they were asleep on the thin bedding on the floor, snuggled against each other under a bedsheet printed with red and yellow concentric circles. Something moved inside him, and he watched them sleep the way his father would have done, with a smile so tender it almost didn't exist. He would tell them about the actor the next morning when he returned, he would probably bring them a scrap of paper signed by the actor, provided he had not already checked out. *Bismi and Beema, good luck.*

It was still night in the coconut grove that stood

behind the house, and he stepped into the dark alley with the lunch pack tucked under his left armpit, the sight of his sleeping sisters clinging to him like a distant happy memory. From the doorway, his mother watched him go; she would linger there until she was sure that he had exhausted the warren of alleys and crossed the footbridge to the main street. Then she would return to the bed but would not sleep, her ears pricked up for the blare of *Jesus* drifting in from the other end of the island.

By the time he reached the footbridge, there was light in the sky and the river was visible through the estates that flanked Manto Road. The river was a stretch of jade, pale grey fog hung over it like the fragments of clouds the sky had dripped overnight. As he walked past Riverview Salon, its shutters down and painted with corrugated faces, he thought of Bina Bomb and her dough-coloured thighs, and imagined her asleep on the red bar stool, her bosom resting on the counter.

The ecologist was at the pier, waiting for the boat; on some mornings the boat brought in parcels for him, wrapped in burlap and secured with plastic straps, and Latif wondered if the Camp Office, the bunch of Blue Shirts and the consignments from the mainland hinted at a new expiry date for the island, which was much earlier than twenty years, probably the next year or the year after that. But the pier side of the island looked intact, and Latif decided to make a trip to the marshes the next day, to check if the last line of mangroves had already gone.

Stella was sweeping the fallen flowers into a little mount under the gulmohar, and her smile reminded him that he had to cook up a story for lunchtime. A story in which Ibru performed acts of bravery unexpected of a seventeen-year-old. She seemed to look forward to his stories, and the stories appeared real even to him once they had been narrated. He believed he had a flair for storytelling.

All the morning he waited to be summoned to Room No. 555, and every time the intercom buzzed he readied himself to take the lift to the fifth floor and add another detail to the story he would carry home in the morning boat. But lesser guests were always on the line, demanding water, extra pillows, or the railway timetable.

During the lunch break, Latif put Ibru on a canoe and pushed it downstream, towards the bend in the river where a convent girl was fast drowning. He hauled her up to the safety of the canoe by her long braid, he would not make the common mistake of offering his hand, that would have risked his own life. A hero's welcome awaited Ibru at the pier; he was thronged and garlanded, and someone even suggested he should marry the convent girl when they were both marriageable age. Much to the girl's chagrin, Ibru declined. Stella listened to the story with a hand supporting her chin, half of her mouth hidden by the heel of her palm. He thought he saw a smile in a corner of her lips when Ibru rejected the girl's hand in marriage and paddled valiantly away. But he heard her click her tongue in disappointment and that steeled him to spin another yarn another day.

Late in the afternoon it started to rain. The gulmohar let go of withering flowers in a flurry, burdening Stella with an extra load for the next morning. Over the patter of rain he heard Stella scream. It was the shameless yell people let out when they came in contact with electric power and only later felt ashamed of. The lodge was abounded in threadbare light switches and exposed wires. He remembered not to touch her if she was still connected to a switchboard when they found her; that was even more foolish than offering a hand to someone drowning. When he saw the manager rushing into the lift, Latif dropped the stack of bedsheets on the counter and followed him. They stopped on every floor, but the scream always came from a floor above until they were on the fifth and Stella's voice was nearer and shriller. Through the grille of the lift Latif saw her standing in the corridor, holding a mop in one hand like a spear, pointing to a door with the other. She looked straight out of a ballet, pointing out the spot where an epic battle was finally won, rendering an elegy in memory of martyrs.

Under the door of Room No. 555, there was a finger of blood. It had stopped moving, though it had not congealed yet.

'Go get the keys from the counter,' panted the manager, pushing Latif in the direction of the lift. But as he turned to leave, the manager held a hand up and said in a small voice, 'Wait, the door is not closed.' He poked a finger at the door, and it creaked open a crack. 'I don't want to see another dead body,' cried Stella and hurried away, dragging the mop behind her as if it were an obstinate child who wanted to linger and see what was on the other side of the door. The manager gave the door a hard push and it fell wide open. At first Latif saw only the sticks of furniture standing like shocked eyewitnesses in the feeble light of the bedside lamp. Then he saw the actor, slumped against the dresser, his left wrist slit open. The manager dropped to his knees and slowly lifted the uncut hand from the floor. 'He is stone-cold. He must have done it hours ago.' He sat still for a long while, his head down, as if mourning for the actor, and then he eased a studded ring off the actor's index finger, the kind people wore for luck, and returned the hand gently to the floor.

Looking away, Latif noticed that the rain that fell behind the windows occasionally caught the light from the neon board of a nearby building; blue and red beads that flew past the windows like shooting stars. It was not until he heard the clank of the lift door bang shut did he realize that he was alone in the room. The manager was already on his way to the lobby, probably to smoke a cigarette and then call the police. Latif turned to leave, his face averted from the dresser, then stopped. The bed was still littered with little hills of dresses, the stack of ironed clothes at its centre, exactly where he had left it two nights ago, the white shirt on top. Where had the actor slept then? In the chair? On the floor? Latif turned to leave again and stopped again. Then he was standing by the bed, quickly picking up the white shirt and rolling it into a tube, its sides looking like jelly roll cakes. He slipped it under his waistline and, careful not to step on the pool of blood, headed out of the room.

Stella had already called it a day. It made Latif uneasy that he would not see her for the next thirty-six hours or so. He would have expressed his shock to her, or his grief, or both. That would have alleviated his shock, or grief, or both. But she had left without a word. He had a bigger story to carry to the island now, but when he felt the coldness of the rolled-up shirt against his abdomen, he knew he would not utter a word about meeting the actor.

The shirt was so soft it stuck to his waistline like an extra padding on his trousers. He didn't even have to lean a bit to hide its presence on his body, but he forced a stoop into his person as he staggered around the lobby. The manager and the man who replaced the manager on certain nights were behind the counter, making calls and talking in whispers. Latif found himself unable to sit down. The uneasiness he had felt at the absence of Stella had grown into a high degree of disquiet. The knowledge that the last boat to the island was due in fifteen minutes made him homesick. He went to the counter and waited for the manager to end the call. 'Can I go home?' he asked hesitantly when the manager hung up. 'I am not feeling well.'

The manager was too busy to shout at him, he pushed his lips out and nodded in the negative. They heard vehicles enter the compound, the doors bang shut, the gravel on the drive crunch under busy feet, voices approach. Latif crossed his hands across his chest and stood straight, like a superhero. He remembered the white shirt had the head of a deer embossed on the pocket. He remembered it had impressive antlers.

10

*T*he mirror was broken in the middle. His face was split into two, a crack running diagonally across the bridge of his nose. He had seen pictures of sad faces broken like that, as if those who faced the mirror had momentarily lost their minds and punched their reflections into a jigsaw puzzle. But he didn't know what level of unhappiness such pictures represented. The mirror he held—an old, oblong piece his mother had bought from a fairground—had only one fracture that climbed from the left-hand bottom to the top right like a graph.

He held the mirror at arm's length and saw that the white shirt was made almost to his measurements, a bit slack around the shoulders and a few inches long for his height but otherwise tailor-made for him. All the shirts he owned were either striped or chequered, and suddenly seemed either very garish or somewhat gaudy. The pure white shirt made him look a bit like an inmate of the island's seminary. He brought the mirror closer to his chest and held it at an angle to see the logo on the pocket. In the poor light, the mirror reflected the antlers so badly that he had to run his fingers over the pocket to ensure that the deer had not shed them in transit. He had buttoned the shirt all the way up to the neck, done the cuffs and tucked the ends under the trousers, something he had always been shy to do. Now he was just short of the Bible under his arm to be mistaken for a novice. He considered marching out and surprising his family, but he needed a story to justify what he thought as the height of sartorial elegance.

Hanging the mirror back on the wall, he lay down on the narrow bed. He hadn't slept a wink the previous night, which he had spent on the bench in the lobby, sitting up, his fingers curled tightly around the edge of the seat, his chest pushed out as if he were battling a serious bout of wheezing, while the lift took people to the fifth floor and back. Shortly after midnight he caught a glimpse of four men carrying a stretcher up the stairs, the lift being too small for four men and the stretcher. A long time afterwards, they carried the body into a waiting ambulance that rolled out of the compound blinking its beacon but not sounding its siren. The sky hadn't started to grey and the birds in the gulmohar hadn't started to chirp yet when, tired of waiting, he left the lodge. He did not take the shortcut, but strolled down the road that circled a row of ancient buildings and led to the tall gates of the jetty. It was too early for commuters, it was even too early for the man who sold tickets from a small wooden booth. Latif sat under the lone shining lamp and watched the wind rustle the curtain of morning glory on the rusting dredger's window. By the time the silhouette of *Jesus* appeared in the distance, his eyes were throbbing with wakefulness, his senses all muddled-up, and he could not decide whether he was at the jetty or at the pier. With the river rippling in the wake of the approaching vessel, the two boat landings, separated by an olive waterbody, looked the same. And now, lying on his bed, one part of him numb, the other jumpy, he thought of the old man sitting next to him on the boat. He had a lush crop of hair on his earlobes, and he held the newspaper, crisp from the press, away from his body and murmured the news to himself. On the lower half of the paper, Latif saw the actor's smiling photograph beneath a bold line which announced his death on a black band. When the old man read the news out, Latif eavesdropped. But a few lines into the report, his fellow passenger lost interest in the dead actor and moved to an inner page.

Latif had a long spell of deep sleep, the kind that left you slobbering onto the pillow, the kind that ran a train of dreams up and down the tracks your tired mind had laid out through unaccustomed landscapes. The room now hoarded shadows that were longer than his bed. The same sense of disorientation, which had overwhelmed him that morning returned. He couldn't now decide if it was day or night, if he was safely home or stuck in a strange place. For a long moment he did not recognize the shirt he was wearing, he did not remember the series of events that had him lying on a narrow bed in a stranger's shirt, buttoned all the way up. When the moment of indecisiveness passed, he shuddered; he saw the dresser in Room No. 555, then he saw the actor's body being interred, shirtless. He felt a sharp jab of guilt, a severe pang of anxiety, and a strong swell of fear. He disrobed himself, compressed the shirt into a little roll and shoved it under the mattress. That gave him a considerable sense of relief, but it didn't last. He had stolen many things in the past; he had stolen candies and coins many times. The guilt of stealing candies lasted only till they melted in his mouth, of stealing coins till they were spent in the market. But this time the guilt and disgrace would cling to him forever, he knew that from the sadness which gathered around his eyes, and he was almost sure that his father's photograph was waiting for him on the living room wall, the accusatory look in his eyes so intense that Latif would want to hang a nicer picture in its place.

As if in penance, he sat still on the bed with his hands between his thighs as the room grew darker around him. He stood up only when it occurred to him that he didn't have to live the rest of his life bearing the burden of shame and the sin of stealing from a dead man. He pulled out the folded shirt from under the mattress, now flattened by his weight, and when he slipped it under his waistline he remembered the first time he had done so. It was just a night ago, but it was beginning to look like a crime he had witnessed, not committed, a long time ago.

The coconut grove was already steeped in the gloomy light of the setting sun. He squatted by the river, like he always did with the fishing reel, and when he was absolutely sure that only the river was watching him, his hand went to his crotch—but as he was about to pull the shirt out, a houseboat appeared round the corner. The Blue Shirts stood on the deck, holding beer bottles and pointing accusatory fingers at the bank. They looked at him, then they looked sharply away, suspecting him to be emptying his bowels in the open. He pretended to be fishing with an invisible bait, waiting for an imaginary pearl spot to nibble at the fictitious earthworm, but it was too late, no-one was looking in his direction anymore. A long time after the Blue Shirts had disappeared from sight, he whipped the shirt out and quickly submitted it to the current. The pleated rim of the river hurriedly soaked the linen and then the force of the tide opened the shirt, the sleeves unfurled and fell to the sides. It stayed in the water as it would have stayed on a hanger, the body straight, the sleeves by its side. He watched it slowly float away, his ears tuned for the throbs of the next houseboat, and when it had finally swung out of view around the bend near the marshes a calmness took hold of him, as if he had safely buried a corpse and built something indestructible over it, erasing all the evidence of a murder he had committed in the spur of the moment.

In the neighbour's living room, the armchair in front of the television was occupied by the old lady who was thin like a pencil, flabby flesh hanging on her limbs like dewlap. Nobody else was at home, which meant Latif could watch anything he pleased, sit wherever he wanted until the man and the lady of the house returned. Partially blind and partially senile, the old lady occasionally mistook him for her grandson and ran her fingers through his hair. He felt faintly guilty about pretending to be someone she doted on, but her trembling hand on his head made him feel good and sad at the same time, and he feared she would withdraw her hand if he told her that he was not who she thought.

He sat down on the floor, his feet away from the carpet as he had often been reminded in a stern voice, but he defied the other rule of not touching anything in the house and picked up the remote. He flipped through the channels until he found the one that played movies back-to-back. And, predictably enough, the dead actor was there. He was in a doctor's coat, holding up an x-ray sheet to the light streaming through a window, and tapping on a torn ligament with the end of a pen. Latif remembered the bunch of syringes under a pillow, the actor diagnosing his own condition, as if playing a doctor had bestowed on him the skills of a real one. He changed the channel, and he was surprised to see the manager's doppelganger on the screen, doing a somersault on a confetti-covered pitch in slow motion.

The next morning, he stole a glance at the manager's hands while signing the muster roll to see if he was wearing the actor's ring. He was not. Probably he, like Latif, had thrown the loot away when nobody was looking. The lunchbreak was a quiet affair; Stella ate with her eyes lowered to the lunchbox, chewing absently. He wondered if he should tell her what he had witnessed in Room No. 555 after she had left the passage in a half trot, hauling the mop behind her. He thought of telling her how the manager had sat by the actor and plucked the ring off of his finger. But the next moment he realized that he dreaded talking about that day as much as she loathed hearing about it. That day had changed his life forever. He wanted to start a conversation, but he didn't know what to say. He thought of saying something about Ibru. But he hadn't thought up a story. Eating in silence was the best thing to do that afternoon.

11

*L*atif turned eighteen on an off day. Oblivious of having become an adult in the eyes of the law, he sat at the doorstep and watched the rain fall on the cassava plants like colourless pebbles. The stumps of cassava his father had prepared a bed for, and his mother had planted a month after she had come out of the forty-day religious quarantine, were now four neat lines of healthy shrubs, replanted many times over.

His house never had curtains, it didn't even have windows when he had been small, only a few empty rectangles that had to sit idle on the bare walls for years until Uncle Koya let them take the windows from the house he had demolished to build a new one. Squatting on the doorstep, he listened to his sisters scurrying around to close the curtainless windows as the rain thickened and the wind from the river threatened to wet the furniture. The roof was porous, and his mother deployed empty utensils to catch the raindrops that trickled in through the cracked rooftiles his father had forgotten to change. He heard the plunks that the rain made in pots and pans, the patter it made on the roof. Then he heard his family right behind him, the girls singing the worst possible version of Happy Birthday, and his mother clapping her hands as if he was in a race and he was in the lead. Sheepishly, he rose to his feet and turned to the untimely evening in the living room. Bismi had a plate in her hands, a round plum cake sat on it, topped with a candle that made her jaw glow. Beema was holding a roll that looked like a scroll, wrapped in a foolscap and secured with a red ribbon that she regularly wore to school.

He was officially eighteen. He could vote in the next elections, he could apply for a driving licence, he could do several things he could not have done a day ago. He was glad that they remembered his birthday and thought of celebrating it, but he was also annoyed that they had forgotten all his birthdays until now, until he had become the sole earning member of the family. He found their joy artificial, as unreal as the tears his mother was so easily moved to. He was happy and angry at the same time, and he didn't know how to handle it. When his mother pinched the crust of the cake and tried to push it into his mouth, he recoiled, but she persisted until he reluctantly parted his lips to let the slice in and, as he started to chew, he noticed the wrappings on her fingers and thought of the state of her skin under the gauze—soft and pale yellow with infection. A sharp tang of antiseptic cream stung his mouth. To kill the taste, he turned to the girls, and they shyly sweetened his mouth with brown dollops.

'Happy Birthday,' said Beema, holding the scroll out to him.

He was no longer annoyed, he was curious, no one had ever gifted him as much as a set of name slips on his birthday. Leaning forward, he offered his hands to her, as if to be handcuffed, and she gingerly placed the roll across his palms. In her hands, it had looked as light as a feather, in his hands, it weighed like a little bird.

'Open and see,' his mother prompted.

'Later,' he said, squeezing the roll inquisitively. It felt like a wad of gauze.

'Open it now,' his mother pleaded.

Latif feigned indifference, faked a loud sigh, and then undid the ribbon, letting it fall to the floor; Beema picked it up and tied it to the end of her braid. With a pout of his lips he veiled his curiosity and unwound the white paper slowly, and found something whiter inside. At the sight of the embroidered antlers, his mouth fell open.

'Where did you get it?' His voice shivered as he waved the shirt in front of his mother. But she misconstrued the softness in his voice as a sign of sheer incredulity and, reassured by it, pressed on. 'You like it or not? Tell us that first.' Of course he had lusted after it, otherwise it would not have been floating around the island.

'I like it,' he said unwillingly. He saw Stella hurrying away from Room No. 555, the mop leaving a long trail behind her. He heard her voice, close and clear as if she was standing in the next room. *I don't want to see another dead body.*

'Put it on,' Bismi said. 'I think it will be a bit big for you.'

He ignored Bismi and turned to his mother, anger rushing to his throat like a deep retch, anger that he did not know how to justify. 'Where did you get it? I am not going to wear it until you tell me that.'

Even before she opened her mouth, Latif could guess how the shirt had sneaked its way back to the house. But he still wanted the details, the insatiable storyteller in him demanded specifics.

A couple of days ago, Latif's mother had gone to the marshes to collect firewood. She took that surreptitious trip every now and then, sneaking past Uncle Koya's house in the late afternoon with a hank of coir and a machete. She paid little heed to the government boards that warned islanders against chipping away the vegetation, and she would swing her machete around. She always worked fast and quiet, careful to spare the shrubs in the immediate vicinity of the warning signs. On that afternoon, she was making a bale out of dry twigs and fair-sized logs when a patch of white against the darkening river caught her eye. At first she thought a body had washed up behind the last line of mangroves, and she wanted to flee. But then she saw it was only a shirt caught in the root of a bush, the river rushing through it and making the sleeves shiver as if in a fit of epilepsy. She thought of Latif, only of Latif, as she searched for a pole long enough to reach the river through the wall of twigs. When she found one, she pushed it through the tangle of shrubs and tried to hook the shirt up by the collar. It was several minutes of patient manoeuvring before she could disengage the shirt from the root and haul it ashore. She could not wait to give it to Latif the next morning, when he returned from work with eyes red from the wind and wakefulness, but the girls insisted they keep it a secret until his birthday.

'Try it,' his family chorused. Bismi had fetched the broken mirror from his room and was holding it up in front of him. 'Let's see how you look in it,' she said from behind the mirror.

He already knew how it looked on him, a bit long for his height and a shade loose at the shoulders. But he complied, and as he pulled on the shirt, he dared a quick glance at his reflection, his face cleaved into two by the crack that climbed like a graph of prosperity. He was not sure—he did not know if it was even possible—but he thought he saw one part of his face smiling, the other frowning.

'He looks a bit like those students at the seminary,' Beema laughed.

'No,' his mother said in an irate voice. 'He looks a lot like his father.'

At the prospect of tears rushing to her eyes, Latif quickly unbuttoned the shirt and peeled it off his body and went back to the doorstep to watch the leaves of the cassava plants tremble in rain. Behind him the plops changed their tenor from metallic to fluidic as the pots and pans filled up, and above him the patter thickened and thinned in sync with the mood swings of the rain.

When the rain stopped and the sky cleared up, his mother asked him to put on the shirt again and comb his hair neatly. 'We are going somewhere,' she announced.

'Where?'

'Somewhere,' she said and went to the girls' room to get dressed.

He looked at his sisters for an answer, but they were seemingly clueless.

'Where?' he insisted.

'I think she is taking you to see a girl since you are eighteen now,' Bismi said.

Did the eighteenth birthday qualify boys to be husbands? He knew twenty-one-year-old husbands and eighteen-year-old wives, but he never imagined he could be the youngest groom on the island. He sensed something warm at the base of his throat, something so pleasant he forgot to fake repulsion. He thought it was mandatory to protest when matrimony was mentioned, but he found himself unable to work up mock anger. The image of a girl lying in his bed and waiting for the blare of *Jesus* to filter in through coconut groves made his heart ache, the thought of her waiting for him at the little wooden gate turned his eyes bright with longing. He went to his room to part his hair neatly at the centre and comb the locks to the sides, where they hung over his ears in oily curls, then he patted some talcum powder on his cheeks and thickened the trace of a moustache with an eyebrow pencil. His fingernails were long and a sickly yellow at the tip. There was something sexually wrong about the long fingernails of men, they suggested a painful interference. He quickly clipped them, and then pressed his fingers to his nose and took in the warm stink of the quick. When he put on the white shirt, he didn't feel any guilt. He tucked in the shirt and felt like a new man.

His makeover pleased his mother. But the girls didn't look even remotely impressed. 'Undo the top button,' said Bismi. 'It will make you look less like a seminary student.'

'He doesn't look like a priest,' his mother said. 'He looks a lot like his father.'

Latif plucked lilac flowers from the fences as he blindly followed his mother down the warrens of alleys that twisted and turned as ludicrously as in a game of help-the-rabbit-get-to-the-carrot. He plucked them off absently and dropped them before taking the next step, as if leaving a floral trail for them to trace their way back home. Where they were heading to he still didn't know, and he didn't have the temerity to ask—his mother had acquired a kind of roughness he was not familiar with. He hoped they would stumble upon a relative or two, and she would be forced to disclose the destination and, when probed further, the purpose of the journey. But only strangers crossed their path until they reached the footbridge.

'Where are we going?' he finally asked her as they passed the seminary which looked to him like a factory where they made silence in different quantities – in sachets, stand packs and big brown cartons. Novices were nowhere to be seen, so Latif could not check how closely he resembled them in the stolen shirt.

'Act your age when you talk to them,' she snapped. 'Or keep quiet. I will talk.'

He knew most of the houses that lined the road, they were big or of moderate size, and he doubted if any of them would accept him as their son-in-law, unless they had a daughter with a seriously sullied past. He was relieved that his mother didn't lead him into any of them. Probably there was a house that sat at the end of a worn path running to the river, a house as small as his own, sheltering a girl who was prettier than the ones who went to the convent in the mainland. The clouds, nearly the colour of the river, hung low; they had left home in such a hurry that the need for an umbrella had been overlooked. The surliness of the sky got him worried; meeting a girl for the first time in wringing wet clothes was perhaps the worst way to meet a girl for the first time. His mother, probably prompted by the rainclouds, accelerated her pace, and he detected in her strides a stubborn urgency that he had never noticed in her before.

When they had left the last of the houses behind and the pier came into view, he began to wonder if they were actually expected at his future wife's house. The thud of cashew nuts being cracked open approached them like a crude piece of music, and a new possibility started to nag him. A girl who worked at Quilon Cashews? He knew all of them; most of them were ugly as sin, and the youngest one should be as old as himself. But his mother ignored Quilon Cashews and marched on and would not stop until they were in front of the Camp Office. She gave it an almost angry look. The rain had made the new paint on the walls look newer. She pushed the gate open and strode resolutely down the gravel drive, Latif almost trotting to catch up with her.

The interpreter sat in the veranda, reading a book, and Latif felt instantly that the man was making good use of his free time by learning another language. He ignored the footfalls on the gravel and continued to read and didn't look up until they were standing at the foot of the short flight of stairs, Latif's mother clearing her throat for his attention. 'Yes?' he asked, scowling mildly.

'We have come to meet the person who is in charge of this office,' she said, and Latif wondered again what made his mother so agitated. Did one of the Blue Shirts whistle when Bismi passed by?

'Why do you want to meet him?' the interpreter asked, putting the book away.

'Call the person who is in charge of this office,' his mother repeated. Her voice had hardened further. On the wall behind the interpreter Latif noticed a big picture of the bra-shaped island, staked lavishly with blue and red thumbtacks.

'Tell me the reason first,' the interpreter said in a calm voice. He was no longer scowling.

'Call him first,' she said, raising her voice, a finger pointed at the open door.

'Please,' the interpreter said, flapping his hands to calm her down.

A bunch of Blue Shirts came out to the veranda

and looked at the mother and son with the same level of interest with which one would watch a street play, detached yet involved. Latif's mother could not decide which Blue Shirt to vent her anger on, if that was what she had come for. Her eyes were still flitting from face to face, deciding, when the ecologist strolled out, the pipe dangling from the corner of his mouth.

'He is in charge,' said the interpreter.

Latif's mother placed a hand on the boy's spine and gave him a light push. He lurched forward, surprised, and then steadied himself and smiled inanely at the graphic earth on a blue shirt.

'Tell him my son has turned eighteen today.'

'Happy birthday,' the interpreter said.

'Ask him to give my son a job. It is because of these people that he has lost his father.'

The interpreter thought for a while before talking to the ecologist, and he thought longer before translating what the ecologist had said with a series of expressive shrugs. 'He is saying this office employs only ecologists and geologists. Is your son either of them?'

She looked briefly at Latif, as if to ask him if he *was* an ecologist or a geologist, by any chance. He dropped his eyes to his neatly clipped fingernails.

'But his father died trying to save one of you,' she

said. 'And this boy has to go to the town to work as a cleaner. And that too for a pittance.'

The interpreter nodded sympathetically, but he didn't relay the story of death and survival to the ecologist.

'Tell him what I have told you.'

With a quick wave of his hand, the ecologist rejected the interpreter's service—he was either beginning to understand the tongue she spoke in, or misery needed no translation. He pushed his lips out and looked at the sky, seemingly counting the clouds. 'I am sorry,' he said at length. 'I am sincerely sorry.'

'He is saying he is sorry,' the interpreter said. 'There is no job for the boy.'

'Because of these people, this sick child has to go to the town to work for a pittance. And you have no job for him?' His mother gave him another push and Latif lurched forward again, less surprised this time.

Sick child? He was never sick, never had any condition and never been bedridden. What kind of sickness was she referring to? Belittled in front of strangers, he turned rebellious, and puffed up his chest to prove that he was healthy and happy, and proud of what he did in the town.

'Please take your mother home,' the interpreter said. 'It is a busy day for these people.'

Latif heard his mother sniffle, and he knew tears were in order. He wanted to drag her home before she turned inconsolable, but he didn't dare touch her today.

'We haven't eaten for two days,' she said, tears in her voice. She sounded just like the lady Latif occasionally ran into at the pier, a hand constantly, almost mechanically, miming for charity. Though he could still taste the raisins from his birthday cake at the back of his mouth, he wondered if he *had* eaten in the past two days. 'Four of us are starving to death because of you.'

Latif saw the Blue Shirts exchange quick glances. From the corner of his eye, he watched the ecologist slip a hand into his back pocket and fish out his wallet. He wanted to make himself scarce, leaving his obstinate mother to deal with the ignominy of being offered alms, but he dreaded to move without her approval, he was scared of her as he had never been. The ecologist held out a little wad of currencies to Latif's mother, and when she didn't move, he offered it to Latif. This is the only way we can help you, he said. I am really sorry.

The interpreter stood silent; a hand doling out money didn't call for any translation, not on this island, not in the distant mainland, nor anywhere beyond that. The sky had started to rumble, not very loud but loud enough to remind Latif that they would reach home soaked if it rained. The absence of an umbrella no longer bothered him; on the contrary, he willed the fat grey clouds to open up; he craved a walk in the rain with his mother, the look of hurt and shame on their faces to be washed away like makeup. He thought wistfully of watching the rain from his doorstep, shivering inside a blanket.

'Please take the money and go home before it starts raining,' advised the interpreter.

Latif's mother took a step backward, and he anticipated another push on his back and braced himself against the thrust. But she didn't touch him, he heard her clear her throat with a flourish, collecting a ball of phlegm in her mouth. Craning her neck out, she spat on the steps with all her might. Then she grabbed him by the wrist and tugged him out of the compound.

'Happy birthday, boy.' He heard the ecologist's voice behind him.

For him, that was the worst birthday of his life.

12

Darkness hung like heavy curtains around the forecourt, and he could almost see them stir in the wind. Occasional bursts of lightning brought visibility back, and the gulmohar stood like a backlit cut-out at the centre of the compound. Emboldened by the lightning arrestors that crowned nearly every tall building in the vicinity, Latif stared through the mottled lobby windows as the skies rumbled and raged over the lodge. The rain, though, was yet to hit the town. It had been raining when he had left the island that morning, Manto's broken nose riotously running. As he passed the Camp Office, the Bald Blue Shirt stopped peeping through a long black tube and smiled sympathetically at him. He looked away angrily, then turned his head to grudge him a smile; he didn't know why he did that. The pier was wet and slippery, and the combination of rain and fog had turned the approaching boat into a blur, colossal and grey. When *Jesus* berthed, it was like a huge shadow being pushed against the pier, and the commuters boarded cautiously as if entering a vessel they had collectively conjured up, unsure of its final destination. With the tarpaulin pulled down over the windows, the boat was dark and smelled faintly of fungus.

Now, as he watched the web of lightning through the branches of the gulmohar, he imagined the river rising and flooding Manto Island, the Camp Office making frantic calls to the mainland for boats. He could see the whole island congregated at the pier, standing in the lashing rain like refugees—they were refugees—his family among them, staring into the distance as the river swallowed the long finger of concrete, and the bolts of lightning illuminated nothing but the absence of rescue boats. The rising water would slowly change the aerial view of the island until nothing was left of the bra shape. The rains had never bothered the islanders, and the torrents had done nothing more to the island than pushing the river a few feet into the estates, retreating when the rain stopped, sometimes leaving dead fish on the grass. But now, in the light of the ecologists' prophecy, Latif thought of the rains with a pang. He dreaded that one rainy morning he would return to the island to find it gone, and *Jesus* would turn around and head back to the town after failing to locate the pier, blaring its horn like a hurriedly composed requiem.

In the distance he heard a transformer explode, and

with a crisp twang the town plunged into darkness. 'No electricity till the morning,' the manager announced, lighting a candle and fixing it on the counter beside the ledger, and in the murky orb of light it threw, he did not look like the Mexican player, he looked like a much older version of himself, one foot in the grave. Latif turned his head and resumed watching the darkness in the forecourt that had deepened since the distant neon lights were extinguished. It was in the light of a particularly long stroke of lightning that he saw two shapes under the gulmohar, hurrying to the lobby. They looked like a figment of his imagination, and he did not expect them to arrive, vanishing at some point between the gulmohar and the collapsible door. They trudged quietly in, and it was not until the manager moved the candle to the edge of the counter did Latif realize that there were actually three of them; a man, a lady, and a little boy sleeping in the man's hands. They looked tired, even their shadows on the wall appeared exhausted to the point of crashing down to the floor the next minute.

The flame of the candle swayed when the manager opened the ledger in which the man began writing his address slowly, as if he was making it up. The smallness of their luggage—a fair-sized handbag that hung from the lady's shoulder—surprised Latif, it could not have contained even a day's clothes for a family of three.

'I am putting you in the best vacant room. But the

lift is not working because of power failure. You will have to use the stairs,' the manager said as he dropped a key into Latif's hands. Latif held the oval trinket of the keychain close to the candle to check the room number. It was 555.

Carrying a candle, Latif led the guests up the stairway, their shadows bouncing on the wall as in a puppet show. They paused on every landing to regain their breath, then laboured up the next flight of stairs, escorted by their shadows. He sensed desperation in their silence, and he thought their clothes smelled of a long train journey. The child did not so much as stir in the arduous journey up five floors, as if he was drugged – or dead.

Latif unlocked the room and pushed the door back but did not venture in and open the windows as he usually did. He did not expect to be tipped, but, as he turned to leave, the lady nudged the man into handing the bellboy a bunch of loose change. 'Leave the candle behind,' the man said in a soft voice. Latif cursed himself for not carrying a spare candle; the long walk down several flights of dark stairs terrified him, and for a moment he hoped the man would volunteer to escort him to the lobby.

A hand clutching the banisters, he braved the dark stairwell. The more he ran, the more he felt like he was trapped in a game of musical chairs, and silence played like a snatch of music in long loops; he feared that the moment it stopped he would sit down on a step and so would the other players, invisible hitherto, and he would let out a long scream that would not stop until the manager came and dragged him through the darkness to the radius of the candlelight. But silence played unbroken, not even a single peal of thunder disturbed its rhythm.

Panting, he burst into the lobby and slumped down on the bench; the manager was already asleep behind the counter, snoring through his open mouth. It took Latif a while to steady his breathing, and until then the candle swayed its flame as if in company. There was something strange about the family in Room No. 555, but he didn't know what—the meagreness of their luggage and the stillness of the child portended something terrible.

When he woke up, the lobby was in darkness. He struck a match and saw that the candle had been reduced to a wick rooted in a thin film of wax. The electricity was still not restored when he left the lodge and, as the boat departed from the jetty, he looked over his shoulder at the unlit town. It looked like the town was destined to live without electricity forever, but the next morning the bulbs in the lobby were shining when he returned to work. The windfalls Stella had swept into a heap were bigger than ever, the gusts being strong the night before. Over lunch, he wanted to tell her about the guests in Room No. 555, but he doubted if she would entertain any talk about that particular room. She had not uttered a word about the actor since she had hurried away to the lift dragging the mop, and he knew she now mopped the fifth floor only out of the fear of losing her job. So, while they ate, he told her about Ibru going to see a girl and rejecting her because the girl had a trace of moustache under her beaky nose.

'But I thought Ibru was only as young as you,' she said.

'Ibru is twenty-one,' he said.

'But you once said he was your classmate.'

He should have told her another story, probably about the Camp Office offering Ibru a job on the virtue of his valour only to be rejected by him on the grounds of the Blue Shirts being drunkards. But it was too late for a new story.

'He failed in every class and when I was promoted to the ninth standard he was there from the previous batch.'

'But I thought you said he was very intelligent.' On certain days, Stella was too tough to handle, just like his mother. On those days she hardly smiled and treated him like he was making up stories, which deeply hurt him. 'Let me judge for myself when I meet him.'

'I don't know when he is coming to the town next.'

'He doesn't have to come to the town. I am coming to your village next month.'

'Why?' He almost sounded offended.

'Isn't there a seminary in your village? And a parish hall next to it? I am coming there to attend a wedding. After the wedding, I will come to your home.'

'When is the wedding?'

'The first Sunday of June.'

After lunch, he sat on the bench and imagined Stella arriving at the pier on the first Sunday of June and going to Quilon Cashews to ask for directions to his home. He thought concernedly about the dirty walls of his house, the moth-eaten window frames, the broken tiles on the roof and the wrappings on his mother's fingers. The intercom buzzed intermittently, and he took the lift to several floors, carrying towels, bedsheets, cold water, the day's newspaper and mosquito repellents. Whenever he went to the fifth floor he passed by Room No. 555, even when he had no business going down to the end of the passage where the room was, and he paused to check the space under the door for traces of blood. There was nothing under the door to unsettle him, but in the silence behind the door, which reminded him of the silence of his island, he smelled blood. As the day wore on, panic rose in him in layers, one fearful possibility stacked on another. The man could hang himself from the ceiling fan, but how would the lady and the child die? He remembered the sound of vials tinkling in the bag that hung from the lady's shoulder as they spiralled their way up the stairway two days ago. Poison? Yes, it would be homicide by poison; no one would think of slitting a child's wrists.

By the late afternoon, he found it impossible to concentrate on anything other than the last moments of the guests in Room No. 555. He wanted Stella to be around when the room was forced open, he longed for a shoulder to lean on when they brought the child's body out. He had never seen a dead child in his life, and the one in the story he had heard in school, the one in which the mother went around the village to bring her son back to life, never left his mind. He pictured the actor sitting by the dresser and watching the couple feed the child a spoonful of poison, cooing in encouragement, as if they were ministering him expectorant. To confirm the deaths in Room No. 555, he walked up to the counter when the manager went to relieve himself. He picked up the intercom and punched busily on the keys, his eyes on the lavatory door. The line remained blank for a while, and just as he heard the first beep, the lavatory door opened. He hung up and got into the lift and navigated himself to the fifth floor. He had never been so certain of a death, so prepared to be shocked.

At the end of the long empty corridor, the sun

streamed through the open window and sketched four blocks of light on the floor, the colour of the river he lived by. He stood in front of Room No. 555, his body stiff with anticipation, a finger shaped like a hook ready to knock on the door, but then he brought himself down to his knees. It was a long time before he could see a spot of light through the keyhole, a peachy glow that he identified as the wall above the bed. He peered harder and saw the edge of a white pillow, the grainy brown of the headboard, and a third object he could not make head or tail of. Then the light dimmed in the keyhole; the bed, the pillow and the peach-coloured wall disappeared, screened off by a blue cloth. Before he could haul himself up, the keyhole disappeared, and he was staring at a pair of brown trousers. The man towered over him, one hand placed on the handle of the open door, the other on his hip.

'Looking for some bedroom scene?' he asked politely.

Latif gave him a half-smile. He saw gravel stuck on the groove of the boot sole as it landed on his right knee and sent him reeling to the floor. The man raised his leg in the air again and brought the boot down on his left knee. The moment the boot was up for another assault, this time directed at his crotch, Latif scampered to his feet and ran to the lift.

Upon reaching the lobby, he left the lift door a crack open so that the man would not be able to hail it to the fifth floor, and the thought of having to climb down several flights of stairs might daunt him from coming to the lobby to hurl abuses at him, or even beat him up. The buzz of the intercom caused him shudder. The manager picked up the receiver and listened patiently, his eyes never leaving the clock on the wall. With a nod of his head, he hung up and went to the storeroom. When he came back he was wielding the broken piece of a mop's handle.

The first blow landed on his back. 'Peeping into rooms?' the manager yelled.

The second hit him on his buttocks. 'Jerking off in front of guests?'

The third and fourth were dealt to his calves, without questions. For a fleeting moment he considered wrestling the stick out of the manager's hands and showering blows on him, on his back, buttocks and calves, as in the jailbreak movie he had watched on the neighbour's TV a few weeks ago. But the moment passed, and he joined his palms at his chest and mimed for clemency.

'Stop!' Stella screamed, stepping in between the manager and Latif, her hands stretched sideways protectively. 'Have you no shame?'

'Ask him that!' the manager panted.

'Have you no shame beating up an abnormal child?' Stella screamed louder.

Latif heard the sound of the stick falling to the floor. He didn't know he was abnormal until that moment. His family had not told him that, none of the islanders had ever treated him like that. Or did they all? Was that why his father named all his ventures after his sisters and none after him? Was that why he was never allowed to sit on the sofa when he went to the neighbour's to watch TV? Was that why they always served him tea in the same old cup?

'Come with me.' The manager grabbed Stella by the elbow and led her to a corner of the lobby, and talked to her in whispers, occasionally stabbing an angry finger in his direction. Stella followed the direction of the finger and looked at him with sad, indecisive eyes. After a while she left, without stopping to chide him for his folly or comfort him for the retribution that had befallen him.

Latif sat on the bench and nursed the red patches on his legs. The broken piece of the mop handle lay where the manager had dropped it, and every time he looked at it, he saw the hand that wielded it, the saffron thread on the wrist. He felt the absence of the thread would have made the retribution less painful, much less insulting.

When the night fell, he dug his hand behind the stack of old newspapers and fished out the cigarette the actor had given him two months ago. He went through the back door and stood under the star fruit tree. The breeze would not let him light the cigarette until half the matchbox was spent, and when, finally, the tip of the cigarette gathered an orange glow he felt a deep sense of achievement. The smoke filled his lungs with a sharp burning taste, and he began to cough like an old man.

13

*H*e walked fast. He almost ran. The whole island seemed to have risen early just to extend him a welcome rife with ridicule, to mock him for the way he walked, the way he conducted himself, for his hairdo, which he loved as much as his sisters loathed it, for his trousers that barely reached his ankles, even for the shape of his dead father's moustache. He glanced around, there were only a few people around, and nobody was looking at him but he still thought he was being laughed at. The moment he disembarked, he sensed something strange had come over the island. He felt the village's treaty with silence had been breached. He heard trees groan in the wind, birds warble angrily and the bell in the seminary toll ominously. The island's acoustic system seemed to have been revamped overnight, just to unsettle him. On the boat, he had refused to look at the convent girls for fear of detecting scorn in their kohl-lined eyes, and on his hurried way home, he didn't smile when the Bald Blue

Shirt waved at him from the porch of the Camp Office.

Only after crossing the footbridge did he think of slowing down. From there, the path that led him home was devoid of people and mockery. In the long, angular alley, he started to suspect if his mother had already heard about what had happened at the lodge; the manager might have telephoned the owner of Quilon Cashews to complain about the bellboy he had recommended, who, in turn, must have relayed the news of Latif's delinquency to his mother through one of his workers. When you erred, the island's communication systems worked flawlessly. He should not have stayed silent and submissive while being flogged, he should have caught hold of the broken handle of the mop and explained why he was peeping through the keyhole. He should at least have told Stella what had driven him to the fifth floor, what had made him kneel in front of Room No. 555.

At the sight of home, his nerves frayed. He broke a switch from the hibiscus bush and stormed into the house and started to flog the first sister he found there.

'Why are you beating her?' his mother cried, standing between him and his sister the way Stella had stood between him and the manager.

'For her grades.'

'But I am yet to get my grades for the year,' Bismi said.

'This is for last year's grades,' he said, swinging the

stick around.

His mother plucked the stick out of his hand, broke it into two and flung it out of the house.

'Next time you will show me your progress report and only I will sign it,' he demanded.

The girls hid behind the kitchen door and began to giggle. He looked around for a ladle to lash them with.

'They will show you the report the next time and only you will sign it.' His mother assured him, knowing well that the school the girls went to never issued a progress card. But the promise pacified him, made him feel important, made him the head of the family once again.

It was while eating breakfast that his mother noticed the welts on his calves. They looked like fading smudges a red sketch pen had left. 'What happened to your legs, Ibru?' she asked.

'The manger beat me up,' he said proudly.

'For what?' she asked.

'For talking back,' he said even more proudly.

'Why did you talk back?' asked Bismi. 'And what did you say?'

He didn't answer her, he was still cross with her for not showing him the progress report the school never issued.

Later that day, on his way to the bathroom behind the kitchen, naked except for a threadbare towel around his waist, the girls saw the red marks on his back and yelled out. 'See, he was beaten on his back too.'

He let out a long hiss when the water, warmed by the sun, touched the welts. Crows were cawing in the curry leaf tree that stood next to the bathroom, the tip of a branch growing over the roofless bathroom, the shadow of its leaves trembling on the water in the drum. Through the cackling of crows he heard his mother behind the wall of thatched coconut leaves, asking where else he was hit. Am I a sick child? Am I abnormal? he asked his mother through the wall, keeping his voice so low it stayed in the bathroom, too feeble to filter through the loose weft of the brittle thatch. He didn't remember being a sick child, he didn't recollect a single instance that qualified him as abnormal. He knew how abnormal children looked like; in his childhood, he had brief encounters with them every fortnight, when his father took him to the government dispensary. The squat little building was white outside and blue inside. The walls of the waiting room were painted in a wavy pattern, drawn with dolphins that smiled apologetically at the visitors. At the centre of the room was a table heaped with building blocks the size of bricks, made of sponge. He remembered a few children from those visits; some had big diabolic ears, some had lopsided faces, and a few had trouble keeping their mouths shut, strands of spittle oozing out from the corners of their lips. He seemed to be the only normal child in that building, which reeked of decaying coconut husk thanks to its proximity to a small coir factory. For him, the trips to the dispensary were nothing to look forward to, except for the pink ice candy that his father bought him after every consultation, and, when the visits finally stopped, he was relieved.

His showering sessions were unusually long, ending only when there was not a single drop of water left in the big black drum, and even then his mother had to rap on the tin door several times before he would think of coming out. But today she let him be, and he wallowed in the absence of urgent knocks and kept moving the soap across his body until he looked like a snowman, immune to the needle-sharp rays of the fierce mid-summer sun. When he came out, his family was sitting on the kitchen steps, and as he pushed past them, he felt their eyes on his back and calves.

That night he woke when his bed creaked. His mother was sitting at the edge of the bed, holding an old inkwell and a pigeon's feather in her hands. She looked like someone who used to be an angel in her younger days, who then decided to retire and rear children.

'You don't have to go to the lodge tomorrow,' she said comfortingly, though a bit sadly.

'Why?' he asked, uncertain if his mother was really there, or if he was dreaming her up.

'You don't have to go there ever again. I don't want anyone to beat up my son.'

'Then?' he asked.

'I will go back to Quilon Cashews. My fingers are much better now.'

She still had wrappings on her fingers, and the gauze was as yellow as ever. But he still did not know if it was a dream or not. Then he saw the light in the next room dim and brighten as the voltage fluctuated. His dreams never had fine details like the play of light or the murmur of feet.

'Or do you want to work at Quilon Cashews?' she asked, unscrewing the cap of the old inkwell. It was the only first aid box in the house, filled with a tacky oil that itself smelled of sickness. She dipped the tip of the feather into the oil and ran it over the welts on his calves. 'I can go and talk to the owner tomorrow.'

He looked at his fingers, they were neat and unblemished, nails clipped close, he didn't want to sully them with the sap from the scorching cashew shells. He didn't want to touch his future wife with fingers as rough as sandpaper. 'No. I don't want to work for him,' he said, and added as an afterthought. 'I will work somewhere else.'

'Yes. You will work somewhere else,' she said encouragingly, and got up from the bed. 'Till then I will work at Quilon Cashews.'

When she left and the light in the next room went out, he regretted more taking all the blows without a word of protest, without throwing a punch back. The regret made the welts sting. He was relieved nonetheless, he didn't have to wait at the lobby anymore, he didn't have to sleep on the bench, he didn't have to travel past the spot his father had drowned every second day. Something moved in his chest at the thought of not being able to see Stella again, she was the only friend he had made in the town, she was the only one who listened to his stories. He closed his eyes and as he drifted to sleep the room shrank to the size of the old lift at the lodge, as narrow and as unquiet, moving down, down, and down, until there was not a grain of wakefulness left in him.

The alarm in his body clock had been set for the same hour since he had started working at the lodge. He got up at a quarter to five, like on every working day, and, intrigued by the blade of light under the door, strolled through the house to the kitchen. Under the sooty lightbulb, his mother was crouching by the stove, cooking lunch for him, as if she had forgotten the promise she made the night before. It could not have been a dream, the welts on his calves still smelled of the balmy oil. He retreated to his room and prepared himself busily so that *Jesus* would not leave the island without him.

Once he crossed the footbridge, things seemed to

have fallen back to the pattern of other days. No one was laughing at him, no one was even paying him any attention, except the Bald Blue Shirt who waved at him, and Latif waved back, though reluctantly. Waiting for the boat, he furtively glanced at the hairless shins above the long white socks the convent girls wore as a part of their uniform and imagined them spending the weekend shaving their legs. He climbed through a window when *Jesus* docked and skittered down the aisle to his favourite seat in the row nearest to the driver's cabin, from where he attentively watched the driver turn and straighten the wheel with charming lethargy. He closed his eyes and pretended to be asleep when the clip-shaped coconut tree came into view and didn't open them until he was certain that the islet had fallen away. So everything followed the prosaic pattern of other days. Even at work. Stella looked up when he passed the gulmohar, the manager glanced at the clock when he signed on the muster roll. He was relieved to see that the key was back on the hook allotted to Room No. 555; his tormentor had vacated, his torment had ended. It calmed him considerably down that things were back to normal. But the lunch break was different, formal and unusually quiet. Stella avoided his eyes and ate in silence. Sensing that it was a bad day to bring Ibru into conversation, he concentrated only on the meal.

'I won't be home on the first Sunday of June,' he said as Stella got up to leave.

'What?' she asked, knitting her brows.

'You are coming to our island on the first Sunday of June?'

She thought for a moment. 'Yes, I am. Why?'

'I won't be home. I am visiting an uncle.'

'I can come and meet your family then.'

'Nobody will be at home,' he said defiantly. 'We are all going.'

14

On the first Sunday of June, Latif paid several visits to the pier to watch *Jesus* pull drowsily in. He skipped the first trip, though; Stella would not take a boat to the island so early in the morning. The four times he was at the pier, the boat was behind schedule, it never kept time on a Sunday. He leaned over the cold railing and spat into the river, just to see if fingerlings would come and nibble at the bubbles his spittle made on the water. When the throbs of *Jesus* funnelled in through the estates, he slipped behind Quilon Cashews to spy on the people who debarked hurriedly and wandered off to the arteries of the island. If he spotted Stella among the commuters, he would run home and herd his family to Uncle Koya's house on some pretext or other. That was his plan, though he could not find a convincing reason to lure his family to Uncle Koya's yet. Aunt Tahira was old and dying, and that was the only reason he could think of, but she had always been old and dying in his memory, and everyone had expected her to predecease Uncle Koya. Probably he would tell his mother that he had heard Aunt Tahira was dashing to the finish line, eager to touch the red ribbon strung across the doors of Jannatul Firdaus with her gaunt chest, egged on by her husband. Once at the plush house, he would have no more reason to worry; bringing his family out of it would be a harder task than getting them in. His mother would end up pickling mangoes, lemons, garlics, and red gooseberries for Uncle Koya's grandchildren, and his sisters would find a way to stretch the visit just to wallow in the little luxuries that the house provided.

Every time the boat left the pier, he thanked *Jesus* for not bringing Stella in. The heaps of charred cashew shells behind Quilon Cashews made him look at his fingers and feel good about not working there. Soon after the four o'clock boat disappeared from sight, he decided to put an end to the irony of waiting so anxiously for somebody he did not want to welcome to the island. Confident that a late evening trip would be as impractical for Stella as the early morning one, he walked home. Later that evening, he went to the marshes to fish, and sat among the mangroves with the reel lowered to the river through a gap between the boulders. When houseboats appeared in the distance, he sprang to his feet, not wanting his posture to be mistaken for the one of a person defecating in the open. Just before the river would shimmer with the pale orange light of the setting sun, a small canoe slid out of a canal that ran between two estates and headed towards the marshes. The water around the boulders rippled as the sound of a paddle puncturing the river came nearer. He stood up and slackened his grip on the reel.

'Hello,' a voice said. He looked up and saw the Bald Blue Shirt seated at the far end of the canoe, holding a sweating can of aerated drink in his hand. The Bald Blue Shirt leaned forward and took a closer look at the boy who appeared to have been recently rebuked and was now sulking, waiting to be apologised to. 'Want to hop in?' He pointed a finger at the empty space between him and the boatman. 'Let's go fishing together.'

Latif pulled the reel back, and the hook landed on the grass, empty except for a knot of waterweed, which seemed to mock him for his bad fishing skills. Beyond 'Hello' he did not understand a single word the Bald Blue Shirt said. But he was sure there was something indecent in what he said, a roundabout invitation to a secret session of debauchery in the Camp Office. He rushed home, the empty hook dancing in the air behind him.

He had wanted to catch a big fish for Stella, big enough to melt her heart and soften her face, then he could explain why he was peeping through the keyhole. The lunch breaks had become quiet affairs and, even when she shared dishes with him, she spoke little. They just straddled the extreme ends of the bench and helped themselves, without so much as a lingering glance at the other. He dreaded she would soon take her lunch sessions somewhere else, maybe to the little room behind the lobby or to the pantry on the first floor.

'I waited for you all of yesterday,' he said, careful not to sound complaining. 'But you didn't come.'

'I didn't come where?' she asked.

'To our island,' he said. 'Yesterday was the first Sunday of June and you were supposed to attend a wedding at the parish hall.'

'The wedding is on the first Sunday of July, not June. You heard me wrong.'

'No, you said it was the first Sunday of June.'

'But didn't you say you were visiting an uncle? Then how could you have waited for me?'

That stumped him, he dropped his head and ate with fierce concentration.

'What's the news about your friend Ibru?' Her voice was soft, like the old days.

He stopped chewing and looked up to see if she was making fun of him. But she looked serious, eager to listen to his stories once again, and he didn't want to waste the opportunity, even though he didn't have a story ready.

'You know what happened to him the other day?' he

asked.

'No, I don't know what happened to him the other day.' In her attempt to mimic him, Stella's face compressed into a mass of childlike features. 'I wouldn't know until you tell me.'

So he told her how Ibru suspected a house he passed every day of hoarding a dead body. It was a small house by a footbridge, where a retired soldier spent the last lap of his life all by himself. When Ibru had not spotted the man tending the garden for three consecutive days—because that was all he seemed to do in his retirement—he played the good Samaritan once again and rang the doorbell. The door went unanswered even after the switch turned warm from too much pressing. He went to the back of the house and tried to prise open a window. Then the soldier was standing right behind him, wielding his rifle. Taking Ibru for an intruder, the towering man launched an attack on him, beating him with no consideration for the boy's age. Ibru took the blows with an equanimity unexpected of an eighteen-year-old, which made the soldier even more furious, and he let out a steady flow of expletives that included passing references to the boy's parents, especially to their private parts. The roles reversed when Ibru wrestled the double barrel out of the old man's hands and launched the counterattack. The soldier was on his knees, blocking the blows with his arms crossed over his face and brokering peace with words of apology.

Latif looked up. It heartened him to see Stella smiling.

'Brave boy,' she said. 'But one doubt. Are soldiers allowed to take their rifles home when they retire?'

'Yes, yes,' he said hurriedly.

'I didn't know that. I have a neighbour who used to be in the army. Let me check with him anyway.'

Did she suspect the veracity of his stories? He himself was beginning to believe it, he saw the Bald Blue Shirt in the role of the soldier, the Camp Office as the house near the footbridge. Probably the role of rifle was a bit too much in the story, it should have been a walking stick or a piece of firewood. He decided the rifle was a mistake, from now on he would remember to censor his tales more tightly. Nevertheless, he was glad that the lunch session had turned conversational once again.

The narrow bench barely allowed him a spell of sleep long and deep enough to produce dreams. But that night it did, and he had a bad dream. He was twenty years older in the dream; everyone on the island, even Aunt Tahira who was not expected to last another summer, was twenty years older in it. They were all at the dark pier, burdened with shapeless bundles and bags that were packed to the zip, their collective glance fixed on the distant outline of the nearest islet, their ears pricked up for the sound of rescue boats. A long time after they had gathered at the pier, a thin wail of a horn reached them, as full of pathos and panic as each member of that midnight congregation, and a blot of yellow light appeared at the curve where the river met the far bank, its intensity changing as the fog shifted. The glowering smudge multiplied and the pounding of the engines grew louder. A whisper of relief spread through the crowd at the sight of the approaching fleet. 'Where is Beema?' his mother asked him in lowered voice. 'Where is Beema?' he asked back, looking around and finding her nowhere. The last time he saw her she was trailing them down the alley, mumbling through her sobs that they had forgotten to take their father's picture from the wall. Did she go back to claim the photograph? 'Wait here,' he told his mother and sister. 'Don't get on the boat till I am back. I won't be long.' He ran home, expecting to see Beema running towards him at some point in his solitary marathon. Only darkness met him on the way. The river had risen up to the platform of the footbridge, and the splashing sound his feet made on the ground grew louder as he entered the alley. The houses along the way stood dark and desolate. The fences had tilted in the high tide and, slanting against each other, they resembled the ribs of a carcass. He reached home breathless, and peeped in through the lattice window, the photograph was on the wall, ready to be buried in the rubble when the tide would pull the house down. He circled the house, crying out his sister's name. When he heard the river rumbling through the neighbour's coconut grove, he hurried back to his family. He was certain that Beema was found and chided for drifting away. The river was now pouring through the handrails of the footbridge, he saw uprooted plantain trees floating underneath, clogging the canal. The nearer he got to the pier, the heavier his legs grew; his turnups were stuffed with slit, his sandals frilled with moss. He saw the specks of yellow light on the river, larger and rounder than before, and as he waited for them to come nearer he realized that he was alone at the pier. The lights were growing smaller, going away. 'Come back,' he howled. 'I haven't boarded.' When the last of the boat skirted the islet and was gone, darkness raced with the river to swallow the ghost island.

He woke up on the bench. He was not sweating, but he still felt a strange sense of wetness about his body, as if he had been walking in a drizzle. His crotch was moist and there was a tiny pool of urine on the bench. He balled up a sheet of newspaper and, with an eye on the sleeping manager, rubbed the traces of the nightmare away.

Long ago, he watched a television report on a massive earthquake in a country he had not heard the name of until then. He stared at the screen with irate eyes, for the neighbour had changed the channel halfway through a movie to watch the news. 'How sad,' the neighbour tut-tutted, sympathising with the little boy in a fur cap who had returned from herding the sheep to find that his village had disappeared from the face of the earth. The boy had big round eyes and a light pink chubby nose, and he sat on the slope of a hill and looked blankly down; where there had been his hamlet there was only a knoll of rubble, a thin trail of smoke threading its way from the centre of the mound to a cloud. Latif could not understand why the boy was not in tears, why he did not look concerned about his next meal or his shelter for the night. Probably it was nothing but a little story they decided to play on the news channel to break the monotony of current affairs, and the boy was a bad actor. A sheep appeared behind the boy and put its head on his shoulder and started to lick his chin. To Latif, the sheep's involvement made it look more like a story than before. 'How touching,' the neighbour said, sniffling.

As he waited on the cleaned-up bench for the manager to wake up, he decided he was luckier than the boy in what the neighbour had taken for a report and he for a story. Earthquakes came without warnings, but an island with twenty years of foreknowledge of its peril lets you uproot yourself and replant elsewhere. The islanders were not as doomed a people as the ecologists had made them believe.

15

Muffled by a country mile, the drumbeats and the sound of bugles seeped in through the open window as he buttoned up the white shirt to the neck. He had not worn it since his eighteenth birthday. As much as he longed to wear it, he did not want to risk its softness and unsullied whiteness for nothing. But Manto Fare was something the whole island waited to attend dressed to the nines, when strings of winking bulbs descended from every tree that lined the road from the pier to the seminary, when the island went to bed well past midnight and woke up late in the morning and yawned the afternoon away. It was the only time of the year when people willingly bought the village thief rum—so that he would be too drunk by the late afternoon to meditate theft. At sunset, the islanders locked their homes and went to the seminary, wandering around the fairground, haggling at temporary stalls, eating at food counters and watching artists perform on a makeshift stage that blocked the view of the 15-foot Virgin Mary and the 3-foot infant Jesus.

Latif dragged the comb through his hair until the locks curved to his satisfaction and sat on the sides of his head like earmuffs. He patted talcum powder onto his cheeks and forehead and ran an eyebrow pencil above his upper lip until his moustache was noticeably present. He tucked in the shirt, on second thoughts he pulled the ends out; the fairground would be abuzz with his old schoolmates, he didn't want to prod the bullies in them awake.

'Undo the button at the neck.' Bismi stood at the front door, blocking his way. 'Else you are not going anywhere.'

Her rage surprised him. She was the meekest of them all, just a year younger to him, the peacemaker in the family, and she had been smiling just a while ago. Such a fit of anger was unprecedented and so unexpected of her that he suspected she had a point. But his mother rushed to his rescue. 'What's wrong with the way he is dressed? It looks fine to me.'

'Undo the button,' Bismi insisted, gesturing at her mother to be quiet. 'Or don't go to the fair.'

He undid the top button.

'Now roll up your sleeves.'

He rolled up the sleeves until his elbows were exposed and waited for her next instruction. But she had already unblocked the front door.

'Bring us some bangles when you come back,' Beema called out when he stepped into the chilly night air.

The alley was stippled with moonlight, and leafy shadows lay at the foot of the fence like the designs that had appeared at the corners of Uncle Koya's obituary advertisement. He stopped where the alley ended and sat on a culvert to regain his idea of sartorial sophistication, doing the button at the neck, unrolling the sleeves and fastening the cuffs. Then he continued to the heart of the island, slipping in and out of inky shadows that covered the narrow path like a threadbare carpet. Crossing the footbridge, he remembered the dream in which he tore through the island in search of his missing sister. The moon rippled in the canal and appeared to pulsate with the distant drumbeats.

The river looked like a painter's rendition of a faraway city, New York maybe, or Venice. Nearer the bank, it reflected the illuminations from the fairground, farther away it twinkled in moonlight. The cornice of the seminary was visible from a long way off, swathed in a purple halo. People were heading to the fairground in twos and threes and in little gangs. He was the only one who walked in the company of himself. The parish hall appeared to move inch by inch to its right as the arrow-shaped serial bulbs darted along its border. The sea of blinking lights and the sound of deafening music made his head swim. When his head steadied, he braced himself against pickpockets with a hand pressed to his right buttock, and blended into the moving silhouettes of the other islanders.

A long line of little stalls sat at the periphery of the fairground, each with its individual music playing from tiny loudspeaker boxes placed among its wares. They traded the same things every year: softies, imitation jewellery, inflatable toys, popcorn, and panacea in plastic bottles. About five fairs back, his father had leased a stall in an inconsequential corner of the ground to sell popcorn in pouches. That was Latif's first lesson in business. He sat on a stool and watched an old chocolate tin fill with crumbled currencies and then go empty as his father flattened the notes between his palms, rolled them into little bundles and slipped them deep into his trunk pocket. Latif was asked to shake a small bronze bell when people walked by. But he held the clapper fast and ducked under the table whenever a schoolmate passed. He didn't know why he did that, whether he dreaded ridicule or discounts he was unable to tell. He believed that three days of trading popcorn had made them immensely rich, and so was surprised to hear his father tell his mother that the priest who leased out the fairground was a crook in a cassock, that he had lost his money again. Every year after his father's death he went to that corner under a sprawling deodar to see what had replaced the popcorn stall. Sometimes a spice outlet, sometimes a food joint, but none had a bronze bell tinkling for attention, they played popular songs instead. As he floated along the string of stalls now, in search of the memory of the days under the deodar, he heard a priest speak from the podium (he could tell it was a priest from the preachy tone and the lengthy inflections he employed as he spoke about the dangers that were slowly eating away the island) and wondered if it was the same crook in a cassock who had looted his father. In the light spilling out of stalls, he saw many convent girls stroll by and nearly didn't recognize them; with their shins hidden under their long colourful dresses, they looked different, less desirable.

He stopped under the deodar and found that the stall had no takers this year. It was just a dark, box-shaped space, filled with the outlines of broken furniture other traders had discarded. The memory of the popcorn stall filled him with sadness and longing. His father had asked him to shake the bronze bell vigorously. He was dinging it reverentially, his father had said, like a pundit. He should emulate an ice candy man. It had to compete with the high-pitched fairground audio and win instantly. And Latif wiggled the bell so devotedly that the effort hurt his wrist and the tintinnabulations his eardrums.

It was a while before he realized that he was not staring

into an empty stall. The tip of a cigarette glowed at the centre of the dark space, and when the glow punctured the darkness at different places, he knew the cigarette was being passed around. He shuddered to think that while he was staring into the stall, pining after the sound of the bronze bell, he was being watched. He turned on his heels and was beginning to walk towards the parish hall when a tall boy emerged from the darkness, a cigarette hanging from the corner of his lips.

'Latif, my friend,' the boy said heartily, extending a hand. As Latif stared back, he wondered if the boy had developed a squint in the years that they had not seen each other.

'Georgie,' Latif said, trying to smile but not taking the hand that was held out to his chest.

On the last day of term, Latif had stabbed Georgie on the back of his upper arm with a pencil and run home. He had been meaning to do it since his first day in high school, but he reserved the comeuppance for the very end. Georgie was so taken aback by the sharp jab of the finely whittled pencil that he forgot to cry, and Latif was equally surprised by the size of the red floral patten on Georgie's sleeve that he forgot to utter the words he had practised the night before. As he ran home, not pausing to regain his breath or looking back to see if he was being chased, Latif found that revenge yielded no contentment, only a heightened sense of fear. A month after the school closed, Georgie's father was posted in a distant city and his family packed up and caught *Jesus* out of the island, but Latif would not venture beyond the footbridge for another month for fear of Georgie still waiting for him at the island square, to stake a sharply stropped pencil so deep into his back that only the ferrule and the eraser stayed out of his body. Nothing would make him wander beyond the radius of relative safety, and Bismi had to go to his school when the results were out and bring back the news of him failing in every subject.

Three years after standing open-mouthed in the school corridor, nursing his bleeding arm, Georgie was offering his hand for a shake. He had grown lankier, and there was a wisp of hair under his lower lip, shaped like a triangle. With a flick of his tongue, he sent the cigarette flying to the ground, and his squint disappeared. The cigarette in Georgie's mouth had disappointed Latif, he had thought he was the only one among his peers to have tasted tobacco.

'Won't we shake hands?' Georgie asked as two boys came out of the dark and stood behind him, smiling shyly at Latif. He could sense how three years had mellowed Georgie down, he was almost moved by the sadness that shone in Georgie's eyes, the nervous smile that played on his lips. He still hesitated to shake Georgie's hand; Georgie had a reputation for crushing palms in the guise of a handshake, he would not loosen the grip until tears smarted in your eyes.

'I hear that you have started working in a hotel or something. Big man Latif. I am happy for you.'

Latif quickly took Georgie's hand and shook it. Georgie gave a light pat on the back of his hand and dropped it without attempting to squeeze the life out of it like on every previous occasion.

'These are my friends from the city. We are here just for a day to attend the fair. Good that we could meet. I even thought of coming to your house just to see you and your mother. I am sorry about your father.'

Latif wanted to shake Georgie's hand again, to squeeze it lightly and ask for his forgiveness.

'We were planning to have a beer when we saw you,' Georgie said in a conspiratorial voice. 'You haven't started drinking yet, have you?'

'I have. But I can't drink tonight. I have to go back home.'

'Good to hear that,' Georgie laughed. 'We have only one bottle between the three of us.' He turned to the boy standing next to him and muttered. 'I asked you to pick up two bottles, but you bought only one. Let's go behind the tree and finish it before anyone comes.'

When the boys disappeared behind the stalls without bidding a proper goodbye, Latif felt he had been excluded from a long-standing coterie for no fault of his own. He decided to wait for them to return, then he decided not to. Uninvited, he treaded carefully over the little humps of rubbish and went to the back of the stalls. Except for the moonlight trickling through the branches, it was dark under the deodar.

'Hold on, Georgie,' one of the boys whispered. 'Someone is there.'

A few feet away from them, a man stood facing the wall, piddling onto the brickwork.

'Don't bother,' Georgie said. 'It's some drunkard. The fairground is always full of them.'

'Finish your beer before anyone comes,' Latif said, happy to play the role of a lookout in this accidental adventure.

'Yes,' Georgie said and turned to his friends. 'Let's finish it before anyone comes.'

'Where is the bottle?' Latif asked in an urgent voice, looking at the empty hands of the boys.

His cheek burned and he swayed on his feet. He was certain that his face had been battered into little pieces of glass. He wanted to check the shards his face had been reduced into, but one of the boys had caught him by the scruff of his neck and pushed him into Georgie's hands. A draught of cool wind touched him on the throat, and he knew his shirt was open at the neck, the top button had popped off. Georgie drew him so close to his body that their lips almost touched.

'You want a kiss?' Georgie asked. Latif smelled tobacco and omelette in his tormentor's breath.

'No,' he said. Georgie must have smelled only fear in his enemy's breath and that must have made him happy. He drove two stiff fingers into Latif's navel and turned them slowly, catching a pinch of flesh between the fingers; Latif didn't feel any pain, the movements of Georgie's fingers only made him think of a Chinese man with a thin drooping moustache, who used chopsticks to make a ring out of a thick hank of noodles. He could not recollect the name of the movie, though. He meekly surrendered himself to the fingers that moved in a tight circle and, even when panic gripped him, he was relieved that his wait for penance was finally coming to an end. He would not put up a resistance unless a pencil came into play, then he would stop being stoic and beg to be let off. He was grateful to Georgie that he didn't let the two boys attack him; in an act of revenge it took a lot of integrity not to bring in outsiders. Georgie pushed him back and held him at arm's length, pouting his lips in sympathy. 'You want to go home now?' he asked tenderly.

'Yes,' Latif said.

His cheek burned again as one of the boys slapped

him from the side. He wanted to check his face again, but his hands were firmly pinioned; he dreaded that from now on every mirror he cared to look at would reflect the same image as the one at home, of a face broken into splinters.

'You want to go home with a knife on your back?' Georgie asked even more tenderly than before.

Why a knife? Latif thought. Could a pencil grow into a knife in three years of unquenched vengeance? He held his tongue; he didn't know what would provoke Georgie further. Standing as steady as his shivering body would allow him, he avoided Georgie's eyes and tried to think of the days when he had shaken a bell reluctantly at a popcorn stall a few feet away from his possible place of death.

'Come closer, sex bomb,' Georgie said, grabbing him by the shirt and pulling him closer. A couple more buttons fell to the ground and the shirt was split open all the way down to his navel. Latif felt a burning sensation raising from the pit of his stomach and rushing to his lips. He felt an uncontrollable urge to defend the shirt. Retching a beastly howl out, he shoved Georgie away and went to his knees to arm himself with a stone. But before he could stand up, the boys threw themselves on him and whacked him from all sides as if they were airing a pillow.

'Let him go,' a voice screamed from behind. They

looked past the tree and saw the man who had been piddling on the wall rushing to them, hurriedly zipping up his trousers. Latif did not see the boys disappear, he just heard their busy footsteps fade away.

'I will come back for you, motherfucker.' He heard Georgie shout.

'What happened?' the man asked breathlessly. Even before he looked up Latif knew the man belonged to the Camp Office. But he was surprised to see the Bald Blue Shirt leaning over him, his hands on his knees.

'Oh, it is you?' the Bald Blue Shirt asked. Even in the dark, Latif saw kindness in his eyes.

Latif picked himself up from the ground slowly and dusted his clothes with the back of his hands.

'Why did they attack you?' the Bald Blue Shirt asked.

Latif did not understand the question; in the absence of the interpreter, he had never understood anything these people said. But he did not want to remain silent. 'Yes,' he said. 'Yes.'

'Your shirt is torn.' The Bald Blue Shirt pointed to his chest and Latif realized that the pocket had almost entirely come off and was hanging like a folded hanky the scouts wore on their chests.

'You are bleeding from the mouth. I think you should go home now. Are you afraid of going home alone?'

Again, he didn't understand anything that the Bald Blue Shirt said. So he said 'yes' again.

'Let's get out of here first,' he said.

They beat a quiet retreat along the back of the stalls, avoiding the fairground, and came out to the street through a rusty revolving gate that overlooked Riverview Salon. The sound from the fairground followed them to the empty street, and they saw the lit boughs of the wayside trees moving in a breeze from the silent river.

'Do you want me to walk you home?' the Bald Blue Shirt asked. 'I don't mind.'

'Yes,' Latif said. 'Yes.' Then he managed a smile at his saviour and ran home. The Bald Blue Shirt did not know if he was expected to trot after the boy or wait for him to come back and tug him along. He stood there for a while and admired the moon sitting above the treeline, then turned and walked back to the fairground, wondering what his own son would be doing at that moment in his faraway home.

16

'What happened to your lips?' Stella asked him when they met up for lunch.

'A spider shat on my face when I was sleeping.'

She touched the corner of his lips and pressed it gently. 'No, this is not what happens with spiders' excrement. Did you get into a fight?'

He shook his head in denial. The previous night his mother had asked him the same question while letting him in. He had come home earlier than expected, without buttons in his shirt, without bangles for the girls, and his mother's relief at having him back before midnight evaporated into horror the moment the door was opened. He stood in the moonlight, a ghost of what he had been barely an hour ago. His face was a mess, streaked with mud, his shirt was a bigger mess, torn and stamped with the mark of a shoe on the chest.

'Did you get into a fight?' she yelped, and the girls woke up and materialised at her elbow.

'I fell into a ditch,' he said curtly and, snatching a towel from the clothesline, dashed to the bathroom behind the kitchen. The crash of water woke the birds in the curry leaf tree, and they twittered short, squeaky protests. Under the full moon, he bathed and bathed until only a cupful of water and the moon were left in the drum, into which he soaked the pocket he had yanked off the shirt.

'Did someone beat you up?' his mother asked through the thatched wall.

'I fell into a ditch,' he repeated.

'Tell me the truth,' his mother implored.

'I fell into a ditch. I fell into a ditch. I fell into a ditch,' he sang out angrily, much to the discomfort of the birds outside.

His mother fell quiet behind the wall, but he knew she was lingering by the bathroom, she almost always did when he took long baths at odd hours. He hated it when she stood guard outside the bathroom, but today her presence reassured him; he could not stop picturing the three boys ploughing a clandestine path through the groves, armed with knives and pencils.

'Haven't you finished yet?' his mother asked after a

long spell of silence.

'I am not coming out if you are going to ask me questions.'

'I won't ask questions,' she said. 'Come out.'

When the girls went back to sleep, his mother sat by his bed and dabbed at his bruised lips with the tip of the pigeon's feather dipped in the balmy oil. He went to sleep with his tongue shoved to the unhurt corner of his mouth for fear of accidentally licking in the smelly oil in his sleep.

'So a spider shat on your face?' Stella asked, watching his face which went lopsided every time he brought a morsel to his mouth and slipped it in through the unharmed side of his lips. 'And you didn't fight with anyone?'

'No, I didn't,' he said. 'But there was a fight near the seminary.' He carefully avoided mentioning Manto Fair, fearing it would tempt her to catch a boat to the island the next evening when the skies and the river would be lit with fireworks.

'Who fought with whom?'

'Ibru fought with three boys. All alone.'

'I thought as much.' She smiled thoughtfully. 'Let's hear about it.'

And he told her how three boys pounced on an

unsuspecting Ibru and how he barehandedly made them lick the dust.

'Nobody intervened?' she asked.

Her hunger for details irked him. Many times bitten, he wanted to roll out a narrative bereft of loopholes this time and make the story sound as convincing as the overnight fight, though he had woken up that morning and found it no more real than something he had watched on TV. The only way to furnish Stella with details was to borrow them straight from the night before.

'Yes, a man from the Camp Office stepped in at the end and sent the boys home.'

'Why did they start a fight in the first place?'

'Because Ibru had stabbed one of the boys with a pencil when they were in school,' he said smugly.

'Stabbed a boy with a pencil? How cruel! Why?'

To tell her why, Latif had to rewind his memories to several summers back, to a little school that sat on the left cup of the island, to the fateful afternoon when his bowels could not wait till the final bell and opened like a creaky door to let a sticky stream out. The stench caused the class to disperse immediately, and when he walked the miserable mile home, his sand-coloured satchel placed on his head so that it would not come into contact with his soiled legs, Georgie trailed him at a safe distance, pinching his nose with two fingers which he took off only when he either wanted to blow a raspberry or to attract a passer-by's attention to Latif's sodden knicker. He escorted Latif all the way down to his gate like a loyal dog and beat a hasty retreat at the sight of Latif's mother perched on the doorstep, skinning coconut leaves for a broom.

Stella moved a hand to her lips to stop a piece of omelette from falling off to her lap; her mouth was so wide open in laughter that he got a glimpse of the underside of her upper teeth, and though he was hurt and angry, he laughed along, pretending to himself that Ibru did exist outside of his being and was human enough to have a fit of diarrhoea at school. It was a while before Stella would stop laughing. 'Anyway, the fight is over thanks to the good man from the Camp Office,' she said, finishing her lunch.

'It is not over yet,' he said in a voice hardened by determination.

'Not over?'

'No. Tomorrow night they will fight again.'

'They shouldn't. Tell your friend Ibru not to pick up any more fight.'

Her words of discouragement did not pacify him, on the contrary, they steeled him to fight again, with more focus, more fiercely. On the final night of the fair, he studied his broken face in the mirror for a long time before sharpening a pencil and slipping it into his trouser pocket. Somewhat certain that he was to return home with dishevelled hair and a face covered in mud, he didn't bother to comb his hair, neither did he apply talcum powder on his cheeks. He put on the clothes he had nearly grown out of. They were destined to be torn and dirtied, and he did not want to be slowed down by his effort to protect them. Feeling armed to the teeth, he marched to the front door.

'You are not going anywhere tonight.' His mother stood at the doorway, striking the same posture Bismi had done a couple of nights ago, her hands firmly gripping the doorframe. Bismi had gone back to her meekest best, and sat on a chair, not wanting to risk his wrath.

'I want to go,' he said defiantly. 'I want to watch the firework.'

'You can watch the firework from the edge of the plantation,' his mother said, jerking her head towards the dark estate behind the house. 'We all can watch it together.'

'No, I am going to the fairground to watch it.'

His mother exchanged glances with his sisters; some coded message passed between them, and the girls withdrew to their room. 'You can go to the fairground. But we will come with you. Your sisters also want to watch the firework. They haven't been to the fair since your father's death.'

Down the deserted alley they walked in silence, dark shapes thirsting for a glimpse of the fairground illuminations. When the tip of the pencil occasionally rubbed against his upper thigh, he paused to change its angle. He didn't think of the firework that would soon paint the skies and the water with different lumina, he thought only of the darkness beneath the deodar, of the three boys waiting for him.

On the final night of Manto Fair, birds on the island hardly slept. Every time the bang of firework whipped the air, trees released frightened flocks, as if it were a ritual the seminary had formed in collusion with nature. They flew out to the river, but in the wake of descending fireballs they always took a turn in transit and zoomed right back to the island, to settle on the trees and to glide over the river again at the next bang.

They had barely walked in through the gate of the seminary when a sperm-shaped beam of light snaked up the sky and burst into a thousand radiant ova. Latif heard men exclaim loudly and children count the glistening orbs as they died down on the descent. A hand feeling the tip of the pencil, he scanned the crowd for his archenemy and his aides. But against the sky that alternated between a floating expanse of melting colours and a static smoky darkness, it was hard to see faces beyond the silhouettes they had turned into. He slowly peeled his mother's fingers off his wrist and took a few steps backwards tentatively to see if she was watching his movements, but she was too engrossed in the pyrotechnics to notice he had freed himself of her grip. As the firework grew in grandeur, he hurried past the stalls, and not until he reached the end of the line did it dawn on him that the boys could be waiting for him in the last stall, and not under the deodar. He faced the dark space bravely, his hand ready to draw the pencil, and stared into the abandoned shop. There was nothing to tell him that the boys were inside, neither the glow of a cigarette nor the clank of beer bottles. Slowly the box-shaped darkness softened, and he saw the stall was empty except for broken chairs and battered crates.

'Georgie,' he called softly. For a moment, he believed he had accidentally stepped into one of those horror movies he had watched on the neighbour's TV, that the secretiveness in his voice resembled the first interaction of a ghost with the new tenants of a haunted house. No one responded. So he drew the pencil out and treaded cautiously down the miry path that ran to the backyard. The trunk of the deodar was so broad that three thin boys could stand behind it shoulder to shoulder, and he was strangely pleased that the Bald Blue Shirt was not standing by the wall to intercede and break up the fight.

'Come out,' he called out to the tree. 'I am ready.'

No one stepped out from behind the deodar. They were probably waiting to pounce on him the moment he peeked around the trunk and wrestle him to the ground. He was not falling for that trap. Dry leaves crackled under his feet as he followed the course of a large invisible circle around the tree, careful to keep a good meter between him and the deodar. The boys would not reach him even if they managed to take the longest possible leap, and that would give him the time to stick the pencil first into Georgie, and then into his friends.

At the half circle, he stopped. It was darker on the other side of the tree, and, if the boys were there, they must be wearing clothes the shade of night and standing pressed against the trunk.

'Come, motherfuckers,' he yelled, his right hand raised in the air, the pencil poised to strike, the fist of his left hand clenched so tight it hurt. 'I am ready for you.'

A train of sperm-shaped flares whistled its way to the sky and multiplied into a hundred glistening balls with a series of crisp crackles. In the flash of its lingering light, Latif saw that there was no one under the tree. He ran to the deodar, howling, and stabbed the whorled trunk with all his might. The pencil broke into two and fell to his feet. But he kept on howling like a sleepless jackal.

17

*F*rom a small shop near the lodge, he bought half a dozen buttons and a spool of thread for the white shirt. Bismi had asked him to bring white buttons, and though they were available in abundance, he picked red. He thought red would look pretty on white, and the novices at the seminary never wore white shirts with red buttons. In spite of the tussle, the shirt was still in good shape, only the buttons and the pocket had suffered and, after thorough laundering which he did personally and with diligence, it turned as speckless as it had been on the day he had taken it to the laundry service. Yanked off the shirt, he now used the pocket as his handkerchief, he shook talcum powder on it every morning before folding it into two and keeping it in his back pocket.

While he had been away buying buttons and thread, the lodge filled up with schoolgirls on a study tour to his island. He walked into the lobby to find it abuzz with their chatter and suppressed giggles. An old nun stood at the counter on the balls of her feet and wrote in the ledger with a hand that trembled so violently that he wondered why one of the two younger nuns who stood behind her did not take the pen from her. A silver chain with a wooden cross for a pendent hung from her scrawny neck and sat on the counter as she worked her pen laboriously on the ledger.

'This boy is from the island you are planning to visit,' the manager said as the nun closed the ledger reverently, as if it were an oversized Bible. The girls and the nuns turned their attention on Latif. 'He takes the morning boat to the island. He will show you the way to the jetty. It's right behind this building.'

'What time does the first boat leave for the island?' the old nun asked. Her voice was as shaky as her hands.

'Five-twenty,' he said. With so many girls around, he felt a bit jumpy, and it was with an effort that he kept his throat from catching. 'The last boat leaves the island at seven-ten in the evening.'

'We are not taking that boat back,' said one of the younger nuns. 'We are staying at the seminary for the night. We are...'

The old nun gave the younger one a hard stare, and the latter stopped in mid-sentence and dropped her gaze to the old nun's crucifix.

When the girls called the old nun Mother Superior,

Latif thought of his own mother, and when they addressed the younger nuns as Sisters he thought of Bismi and Beema. The girls hated the Mother Superior as much as they doted on the Sisters. He could sense that from their whispers as he took them to different floors in the rattling lift, five at a time, and herded them down the dimly lit passages to their rooms. The girls filled the lift with a mildly floral fragrance, but when the nuns stepped in he thought it smelt only of their clean breath, of patina.

'How much of your island is already gone?' the Mother Superior asked when he unlocked the room designated to them.

He did not understand the question, and his silence seemed to have angered her.

'Is your island fast sinking?' she asked.

On his last day off, Latif had a momentary sensation that the river had advanced into the estate, at the edge of which he was sitting with his fishing rod. The bank looked more rugged than ever, and the narrow canal that ran through the estate appeared to flow faster. But the sensation passed, and he reassured himself about the indestructibility of his island.

'It will not sink for twenty years,' he said, sounding like the ambassador of Manto Island's collective willpower.

'Then why the hurry?' she asked the Sisters irately.

'We could have made this trip ten years later.'

Will she last another year? Latif wondered, and he thought the quick glance that passed between the Sisters seemed to hold the same level of scepticism.

The girls turned the lodge as noisy as a school during recess. Their footsteps scurried up and down the corridors, sometimes on tiptoes, sometimes in bold busy strides. Their laughter leaked down the lift shaft like brief spurts of rain, and their shrieks made him long to join them and shriek along with them. Every time he heard the lift grumbling its way to the lobby, he sat upright on the bench and quickly picked up an English newspaper from the stack and stared at the headline, legs crossed at the knees. Shadows fell on the page as the girls blocked the light from the counter in passing. Ephemerally the paper was printed with ponytails, crewcuts, low buns and bobs. But he would not look up until they were under the gulmohar, collecting fallen flowers and wearing them in their hair. He watched them through the window that reflected his face at certain angles. Finally, it took the Mother Superior to come down and whisk them back to the lobby and bundle them into the lift with a finger that she kept wagging angrily. The last girl to get into the lift was the tallest of the bunch, she had long curly hair that reached down to the base of her spine and big eyes that seemed to smile. She put her head around the lift door and winked at him and then gave him a quick furtive wave. Before he could wave back, her head disappeared into the lift and the sliding door banged shut. Long hair, big eyes, a wink, and a wave; he found himself instantly smitten. He hoped she was as poor as she was beautiful. Rich and beautiful girls did not work in his favour as he was poor and not much to look at. He did not mind her being rich as long as she had some physical impediment, that somehow made them equal. But she had not, and so his only hope now was she was poorer than him or, better still, an orphan.

Sleepless in love, he spent the night staring at the stucco vines on the false ceiling. Slowly he started aligning in his head the three-word headline that he had read as many times as the lift door had opened that night. SAFFRON SWEEPS NATION.

He was not sure if he had got the order of words right. So he realigned them. SWEEPS SAFFRON NATION.

He was not yet sure. He reshuffled the words again. NATION SAFFRON SWEEPS.

He was confused. The stack of newspapers stood behind the water dispenser; a couple of steps and he could check if he had finally got the order of words right. But he found the three short words a good plaything, in his mind he tossed them like dice, and they fell in a new formation inside his head. NATION SWEEPS SAFFRON.

The wail of the lift woke him up. He had fallen asleep at some point in tossing the three words up and letting them fall in new patterns. The alarm sounded like a long ugly whistle full of carnal urgency. Latif heard someone bang on the lift door and shout for help.

'It is those girls,' the manager said sleepily. 'The lift is stuck.'

Latif grabbed a torch and tore up the stairwell, pausing on every floor to shine the torch into the lift shaft and, spotting nothing other than the counterweight, bounded up the next flight of stairs. On the fourth floor, he saw heels and hems of many night gowns, on the fifth he pressed his face to the shutter and peeked down. Stalled between two floors, the lift looked like an overcrowded bunker, the girls peering up at him expectantly. The girl who had winked and waved at him stood closest to the door, her big eyes were pools of paranoia, brimming over. He wanted to slip a hand through the grille and wipe her tears.

'Get us out,' she pleaded breathlessly. 'I'm asthmatic.'

He ran back to fetch the manager, and as he spiralled down the dark stairwell it struck him as a good thing that she had weak lungs; her ill-health compensated for his penury. On the last flight of stairs, he saw the manager walking up lazily.

'We have to call the fire force,' Latif said urgently.

'Why? the manager asked. 'Your grandmother fell into a well?'

'No. The lift is stuck.'

'This is the fire force,' he said, holding up a screwdriver and continuing up the stairs. The lack of panic in his voice enraged Latif, and the way he dragged himself up the stairs made him want to shout at him. He willed to run up the stairs and reassure the girls that help was on its way. But he did not want to be ridiculed for his haste, and so followed the manager meekly.

The Sisters were standing on their knees by the lift, whispering angrily to the girls through the grille. They shrank their bodies to make space for the manger. But he stood away from the lift and used the screwdriver to count the heads that looked up at him anxiously.

'Only nine passengers?' he asked. 'There is enough space for nine more.'

'Please get us out,' the tall girl cried. 'I am asthmatic.'

'Be quiet, Paru,' one of the Sisters placed a finger across her lips. 'Don't wake Mother Superior. If she comes to know about this, she will happily cancel the trip to the island.'

Cursing under his breath, the manager jabbed the screwdriver into a hole and rolled the shutter aside. The girls threw their hands up at him as if they were hungry refugees begging for food. But he shook his head and stepped away, leaving the Sisters to pull the girls onto the landing one by one.

Latif did not know how long he slept after that. The sound of the lift growling down to the lobby woke him. He ran to the bathroom to wash his face, drag the comb through his hair until the locks sat above his ears like brackets and then dabbed at his face with the pocket-turned-hanky, transferring the thin sheets of talcum powder onto his moist cheeks. Then he rubbed away the creases on his shirt with his palms.

By the time he was back, the entire excursion had congregated in the lobby. Paru sat on the bench, tapping her foot on the floor. He owed her a wink and a wave, but he found himself powerless to give her so much as a glance.

'Where is that thin stick of a bellboy who will lead us to the jetty?' the Mother Superior asked.

'He is standing right next to you?' said the manager.

'Oh,' she said, turning to him, and the girls broke into a laughter. 'Can't he take us to the jetty then?'

Walking as soldierly as he could, Latif led the excursion down the dark path. The girls walked behind him in crocodiles, chattering, the nuns brought up the rear in stern silence. He felt in charge, the only man who could guard the forty-odd women against the dangers that might lurk in the dark. Maybe at some point in their journey to the island, someone, most probably one of the Sisters, would ask after his family and he would tell them he protected three women at home, that he had always been entrusted with the task of guarding women. He felt the eyes of Paru on the back of his head, eyes that shone with gratitude and admiration. He longed the path to the jetty to be infinitely long, but it seemed to have shrunken overnight by many a furlong.

A lone murky yellow light shone above the jetty building and, at the first sight of the river, the Mother Superior overtook the pack and led the way.

'Hurry,' she called out, hurrying towards the abandoned dredger. 'Our boat is here.'

'That is a dredger,' Latif said. 'Not a boat.' He expected the girls to erupt in laughter, but no one let out so much as a giggle.

The wind from the river was particularly cold, and the girls and the Sisters formed a tight huddle near the ticket booth. He leaned against a pillar not far from them, his hands raised and wrapped around the clammy column, striking a pose almost like the figure on the crucifix the Mother Superior had on the silver chain. She was sitting alone on a cold bench and praying the rosary.

'*Jesus* will be here soon,' Latif said as a sphere of amber light appeared in the distance, followed by feeble thuds of the engine.

'What?' the Mother Superior snapped at him. 'What did you say about Jesus?'

'Jesus is the name of the boat,' a booming voice said. Latif shuddered and turned his head to find the Bald Blue Shirt standing behind him, only that he was wearing a red shirt.

'Sorry,' the Mother Superior told the Bald Blue Shirt. 'I thought this boy was referring to the good shepherd.'

'Not your mistake,' he laughed. 'When I was new to this place, I, too, was surprised that someone had thought of naming a boat after Jesus.'

While *Jesus* made slow progress to the jetty, Latif listened to the Mother Superior and the Bald Blue Shirt chat as if they were old friends filling each other in on the lives of mutual acquaintances. Though he did not understand a word they said, he was certain that they talked about the bra-shaped island and its end that approached as slowly and surely as the incoming boat.

18

The girls sang as if the boat were a church and they were the choir, and their song wrestled with the whirr of the engine and the gusts of wind as *Jesus* picked up speed and moved fluidly through blinds of fog. By pressing his thighs together and collapsing his shoulders, Latif turned himself into a thinner boy, so that his body would not make contact with the passengers he shared the first row with. The Mother Superior sat on his left and the Bald Blue Shirt on his right. They, too, sat stiff, their bodies compressed, either sensing his aversion to be touched or because of the chilly wind, and they all stared into the driver's cabin demurely.

Where the river forked and the boat turned left to head east, fog lifted and the sun appeared above the first of the five islands that stood between Latif's work and home. A pale pumpkin light spread through the boat, and the girls now sang in a lower pitch. Latif felt a pair of big eyes on the curls that covered his ears. While boarding, he had been nervous at the prospect of sharing a row with Paru, and he was both relieved and disappointed when the Bald Blue Shirt took the aisle seat next to him. He had not turned to look at Paru since then, but he had been feeling her eyes on him in the grey feathery light inside the boat. Now brave enough to return the wink he owed her since late last night, he looked over his shoulder and found her fast asleep, her head on the lap of a Sister. Not just Paru, nobody was paying his curls any attention. He returned his gaze to the driver's cabin feeling that the back of his head was the most neglected part of his anatomy.

The islands passed like milestones, they were not fully awake yet, the chimneys still had not started to smoke. Occasionally Latif spotted a man or two perched on the edge of the bank, brushing their teeth with fingers dipped in powdered charcoal.

'What does this endangered island look like?' The Mother Superior leaned forward so that she could address the Bald Blue Shirt directly.

'It is oval in shape,' the Bald Blue Shirt replied. 'From the air, it looks a bit different, though. Like...,' he fumbled for the right words, smiling. 'Like a lady's blouse. A sleeveless blouse.'

'That will interest the girls. They would love to see it from the air.'

To hide his smile, the Bald Blue Shirt turned his head away from the nun and stroked his left earlobe. 'We have aerial pictures of the island at our office,' he said at length. 'You are welcome to come and see them if you want.'

'Of course, we will.'

Shortly after the penultimate island of the archipelago disappeared from sight Latif closed his eyes, as he did every time the boat approached the nameless islet. He would keep them shut for a few minutes and, in the night of his closed eyes, he would see his father dressed in the clothes he had worn on the day he drowned, about to close the little wooden gate behind him and walk down the alley for the last time. Latif remembered his father pausing at the gate to open the letterbox that he had strung to it. It was empty; no one ever wrote to him. Then he turned to Beema and wiped the sweat off her face with his handkerchief, which he used to rub under his nose every time he had a dose of snuff, and asked her not to play in the sun in the interest of her complexion. When his body was brought home late in the evening, Beema's cheeks still smelt of powdered tobacco.

Latif opened his eyes when he heard something snap under his feet, a crisp metallic bang that he often heard in the vicinity of garages. The boat swayed violently. Then it stopped, and with a heavy pant, the engine died. The girls stopped singing.

'What happened?' the Bald Blue Shirt asked the driver who rushed out of his cabin and leaned over the deck to look at the bow. Through the crook of the driver's arm, Latif saw a thin finger of oil beginning to spread on the water.

'I think we hit something,' the driver said to himself, stroking his beard pensively. The calmness in his voice worried Latif, he was the one who always rushed commuters with his yells and sent balls of phlegm impatiently into the river every now and then.

'Is it trouble?' the Bald Blue Shirt asked, quieter than before.

'Yes. Trouble,' said the driver in a calmer voice.

A slow coldness crept up Latif's ankles and he realized that the floor had turned almost pulpy. The river was seeping into the boat, filling the grooves between the floorboards without haste. When the driver turned on his heels to go back to the cabin, his rubber shoes squeaked like a cartoon pig, and he looked down and mumbled at his sodden footwear. Latif tried to read the driver's lips, but he could not tell if he swore under his breath or said a quick prayer.

'Why are we not moving?' the Mother Superior asked innocently.

'Some minor technical snag,' said the Bald Blue Shirt. 'The driver is looking into it.'

The driver returned a while later, a set of blanched lifebuoys looped into his arms.

'Those who don't know how to swim can wear these,' he said, dropping them onto the floor. 'Just in case.'

There was a rush for lifebuoys until there was nothing left on the wet floor. The driver went back to his cabin and returned with more, which, too, went like hot cakes. 'No more lifebuoys,' he announced. They were short of three buoys, and the Bald Blue Shirt, Latif and the driver looked not just unprotected, they looked naked.

'You can swim?' the Mother Superior asked the Bald Blue Shirt.

'Not a good swimmer.'

'And you?' she addressed Latif for the first time since they had left the town.

He nodded confidently.

'Don't move around please,' the driver addressed the commuters from the door to his cabin. 'Sit where you are. We will wait for the next boat to pass by.'

Unfortunately, the only boat that plied that particular stretch of river was *Jesus* itself. So they would be waiting in vain. Latif pinned his hopes on a stray canoe or one of those country boats that carried cargo to the archipelago twice a week.

The Bald Blue Shirt took out his mobile phone and

started to punch the keys busily. 'Let me talk to the Camp Office and ask them to arrange for a boat.'

The driver smirked.

The Bald Blue Shirt clicked his tongue and hung up. 'No network.'

The lifebuoy hung loose around the Mother Superior's waist and made her look comical. If the boat did not sink, the girls would probably look back on this morning and have a hearty laugh over the memory of the old nun in a faded buoy.

'Girls, why don't you start *Ave Maria*?' the Mother Superior asked.

The girls sang in a low voice, and after the first stanza the Sisters joined in.

'You too,' she instructed the Bald Blue Shirt.

'No, thanks.'

'And you?' she asked Latif.

He nodded his head in the negative. He was already saying a *fatiha* behind his sealed lips.

The driver had gone back to the cabin shortly after the hymn had started, and the sound of him trying to revive the engine wafted out of the cabin at regular intervals. The engine hummed for a long moment, but after letting out a series of weak throbs it invariably spluttered out.

Latif noticed a pattern; the girls dropped their volume every time the boat shivered with the growl of the engine, they sang louder when the engine fell quiet.

After about a quarter of an hour of waiting for a boat to pass by, of his silent *fatiha* being repeatedly derailed by *Ave Maria*, Latif stood up. 'I will go and get help,' he said, and the hymn stopped. His voice had an intentional baritone to it, and he felt it was his father who was speaking through him.

The driver stopped tinkering with the gear shaft and turned his head to look at him, his eyes were wide open in wonder, his brows knitted in doubt. 'You will go where?'

'To the island,' he said, pointing to the empty expanse that stretched to the east.

'And how will you go?' the driver asked him encouragingly, like a patient teacher who wanted the whole class to hear the answer.

'I will swim,' he said loudly, even though he knew the entire boat would hear him even if he mumbled.

'No, no.' The Bald Blue Shirt sprang to his feet, shaking his head. 'No way.'

'These boys are good at swimming,' the driver said in a tone that suggested he wanted to convince everyone about Latif's aquatic capabilities whilst he was not convinced himself.

'Then let him go,' the Mother Superior said.

'No,' the Bald Blue Shirt addressed the Mother Superior in a mildly irritated voice. 'His father drowned while trying to save one of my colleagues. Let's not risk his life too.'

Latif knew his father was being mentioned, but he did not know what exactly was being said about his sacrifice.

'I have forty-one girls and two nuns to save.' The Mother Superior with a jerk of her head towards the back of the boat. 'Had I known to swim, I would have happily jumped into the water.'

Latif went to the door and positioned himself on the ledge, clutching an overhead rail for balance. He screwed up his eyes at the still river, as if he could fathom its depth just by staring into it. The land could not be far away, clumps of water moss were bobbing by. He was confident of making it to the pier, even if the river took his fortitude as a personal affront and decided to be unimaginably challenging. He gauged the weight of the mission he was going to undertake, it weighed lighter than the pigeon's feather his mother dipped in the oily balm and ran over his wounds. The only thing that daunted him was the inescapability of swimming past the nameless islet, which he had always averted his eyes from. Somewhere on that islet, they had erected a makeshift morgue to do post-mortem on his father and the ecologist. The structure, made of bamboo poles and coconut branches, still stood, though its walls had wilted down and slanted sideways.

'Why don't we give him a lifebuoy so that he will be safe?' the Mother Superior suggested.

'Then he won't be able to swim fast,' the driver said. 'He will go where the tide takes him.'

In preparation of the plunge, Latif patted the seat of his trousers and found that his back pocket was stuffed with his wallet, the packet containing red buttons and the reel of thread, and the hanky. He took them out but did not know whom to entrust them with. The Bald Blue Shirt held a hand out to him, and Latif placed them carefully on his palm, one item at a time. He had a fleeting image of the Bald Blue Shirt handing them to his mother, watched by his sisters. He blinked the image away.

'Are you sure about this?' the Bald Blue Shirt asked, a finger pointed at the river.

As usual, Latif did not understand his words, but he nodded and, as an afterthought, smiled.

'I will keep these safe for you,' he said, pressing Latif's belongings to his heart, as if promising to honour the boy's last wish.

Latif faced the river again, the vast waterbody that would one day leave nothing of his island behind.

Beneath him, his shadow undulated like a water spirit coming up to greet him. He stretched his hands out and brought them closer until his forefingers met, and like a flying fish he threw himself into the waiting river. The moment his body dented the surface, he remembered he had not swum in years. The river tasted like a strange quinine, of salt, moss, and raw fish. Swinging his hands with a flourish, he sliced the water with more force than needed to cut the surface and followed what he imagined to be the course *Jesus* took four times a day. The entire boat had its eyes on him, he knew that without looking back, and he fought the urge to cast a backward glance and see the look of admiration on Paru's face. A broad carpet of water moss glided towards him in low tide, and he switched to a front crawl to squirm through it.

The choir was alive again, they probably were praying more for his safety than their own, and just as their voices had turned to a rubbery murmur he heard the engine roar to life. 'Come back,' the driver yelled. 'The boat can move now. Let's go.'

Never in his recent memory had Latif felt coming so close to a certain glory and then being dragged back to the prosaic insular life. He took a reluctant turn and swam towards the pulsating boat, spewing the river back into the river.

19

*H*e tore through the island square like a walking laundry line, dripping the remnant of his aborted adventure to the narrow road going home. The taste of the river still lingered in his mouth, as absinthian as the memory of the moment when the boat had coughed up a ribbon of smoke and he was so inconsiderately summoned back. They hauled him onboard like a dead body and sat him on the floor, but he quickly sprang to his feet, even though he had wanted to rest till his breathing levelled out, and leaned against a pole with his hands inserted into his trouser pockets, legs crossed at the ankles. Staring thoughtfully ahead, he secretly used his fingers to push his testicles back into his underwear while the boat chugged uncertainly up the last mile.

The resurrected *Jesus* took about five minutes to get to the pier; a shiver ran up his spine at the thought that it would have taken him about half an hour to be ashore, but he still felt discriminated against; he had been offered a chance to do something his father had perished doing, and then he had been deprived of it.

A fat cloud hung low over the island and lent it the look of a snow globe accidentally filled with tropical trees. The girls erupted into a war cry and scampered for their luggage as the island grew bigger in the window of the driver's cabin and the cloud disappeared above the boat's roof. Latif caught a glimpse of his shadow on the water, airborne, as he leapt over to the pier when the boat was still a few feet short of the dock. He did not wait for anyone; he dreaded someone would belittle his heroic act, albeit unfinished, by slipping a folded currency into his hand. But no one asked him to stop, no one even threw a word of gratitude in his direction.

On the footbridge he paused to wring the end of his shirt and the cuffs, and then to puff up his hair by running his cold fingers through the locks like a comb, using the greasy canal below as the mirror. He could not decide why he was heartbroken, why he had a lump in his throat, why his legs wanted to carry him home while his mind willed him to return to the pier. When a wind blew down the canal and made him shiver, he remembered home and resumed walking. The summer sun had warmed his face to a slippery dryness, but the wet clothes sat on him like polythene, flat in places, bubbled in patches.

At the mouth of the alley, he saw his mother hurrying

towards him. The boat was well behind schedule, and she was heading to the pier in search of him. She looked surprised to see him, for she had not heard the boat blare; *Jesus* had docked quietly, as if ashamed of stalling in midwaters, not wanting to attract the waiting commuters' ridicule.

'Why are you wet?' she asked.

'It was raining,' he said impatiently.

'Raining where?'

'In the town.' He walked faster to avoid the next question, but she caught up with him and tried to dry his hair with her shawl. Jerking his head away, he walked even faster.

After a long shower and a quick breakfast, he went to bed. Even though he had slept only in short spells the previous night and was tired from swimming—more from swimming back to the boat than swimming away from it—he stayed wide awake.

'Have you bought buttons for your shirt?' Bismi came into the room with the white shirt and a needle as he lay staring at the ceiling. He pointed at the little brown packet that sat on the windowsill.

'Red buttons,' she exclaimed. 'I asked you to bring white ones. What is wrong with you?' But she threaded the needle and sat on the edge of the bed to sew the buttons in. 'It's not as bad as I thought,' she said, admiring her work.

The red buttons sat on the white shirt like pretty ladybugs, which made his spirit rise, and he asked his sister to get the shirt ironed. 'Be careful with it. I don't want dirt from the iron plastered all over the shirt.' He knew he sounded exactly like the rightful owner of the shirt, and it surprised him that he had not thought of the dead actor for a long time. He could think of it now only as the first birthday gift from his family.

The river had given his hair more manoeuvrability than oil, or so he thought as he worked the comb sideways from the centre parting. He easily achieved the curls he had always struggled to make, and they sat obediently over his ears, their ends curving like hooks. He saw the symmetry of happiness in the mirror, his smile ended at the crack that ran through the middle but spilled over to the other side. At the prospect of meeting Paru again, he clipped his fingernails, though he was somewhat sure she would not look at his hands.

'Where are you going?' Bismi asked him when he floated through the house.

'To the seminary?'

'You have finally decided to join the seminary?' she laughed, sizing him up in his white shirt. His mother had starched it well and Bismi had pressed it meticulously, and the linen now felt almost like medium-grade plastic. 'Roll up your sleeves, for god's sake,' she said, joining her palms in fake supplication. 'You look like a pastor.'

He paid her little attention and walked on.

'One day I will cut the sleeves at the elbow,' she called out as he opened the gate and stepped into the alley. The sun worried him with its blinding ferocity. To save his shirt and makeup from sweat, he kept switching to the shaded parts of the street all the way up to the seminary gate. Except during Manto Fair, entry to the seminary was restricted, and its tall, silver-plated gate stood like a stern reminder of its need for privacy, guarded by an old man who sat sleeping outside the security cabin. Latif waited in the shade of the biggest tree on Manto Road, careful not to lean against anything that would spoil the pleasant rigidness of the freshly-ironed-shirt.

As he waited for the girls, he thought of Georgie. At some point in the near or distant future, probably on the very day life would start treating him well, Georgie would return to the island with a penknife and stick it into his ribs. He was certain about that eventuality, even of him wearing the white shirt on that night; he could not imagine the knifing happening in broad daylight, he did not know why, he just could not. Georgie would be intent only on hurting him a bit more than he had hurt Georgie with the pencil, but the knife, not being pencil, would slip in an extra inch and do him in. He could bet his life on that possibility. Many movies he had watched on the neighbour's TV had tutored him on dreary climaxes; misfortunes had such an inane habit of striking when life was just about blooming. He did not particularly like those movies, the ones which had tragedy reserved to the very last scene, that if his mother had beckoned him home a minute before the credits came on, he would have run through the dark coconut grove believing that the movie had ended on a happy note in the neighbour's study. He thought that was an unkind way to end a movie, as unfair as a goal in injury time.

When the old guard woke up, Latif mustered up the courage to enquire about the visiting nuns. The guard looked towards the seminary building and then at the summer sky, and then he remembered; the nuns had left a while ago with a group of noisy girls, but he did not know where they had headed to. Latif knew where they could be, and hurried towards the pier, switching sides to walk under the trees. His heart sank when he found only the Blue Shirts at the Camp Office. He turned to go home, the lump in his throat bigger and harder now. A few feet down the road he was stopped by the chorus of the girls drifting in from somewhere beyond the pier. A houseboat slid into view, floating aimlessly as if taken by the wind, and he was not sure if it would dock for the day, but it came straight to the pier and the girls tumbled out.

'Where had you run off, son?' the Mother Superior placed a trembling hand under his chin, and his face shivered with the rhythm of her unsteady hand. 'You did not even let us thank you.'

'Thank you,' said one of the Sisters.

'Thank you very much,' said the other.

'The boys at the seminary are attending an exam today,' the Mother Superior said. Her hand still rested on his chin, but it had either stopped trembling or Latif had quickly acclimatized himself to its unsteadiness, for he no longer felt the tremor. 'So we don't have anyone to show us around the village. Will you be our guide?'

Whenever their help was sought, the islanders first deigned to be frightfully busy for the rest of their lives, only to change their minds at the faintest sign of persuasion. By looking uninterested and saying nothing, Latif just followed the common trait of his republic.

'Don't worry, son.' She squeezed his chin lightly. 'We will pay you for your service.'

He regretted not readily agreeing to be their guide. 'No, I don't want money.'

'Please,' prompted the Sisters. He spotted Paru at the back of the pack, she held up her hands and wiggled her fingers as though telling him that she had worms crawling up her spine and needed his help to dislodge them.

'Yes,' he said. 'I will show you around.'

'Tell us where all you can take us,' said the Mother Superior, letting go of his chin. 'The most interesting places around.'

'The seminary,' he said enthusiastically.

A hum of laughter rippled through the crowd of girls.

'That's where we freshened up and rested till an hour ago,' one of the Sisters said, grinning widely at him. 'Mother wants to know about the local attractions.'

He tried to think of the local attractions; other than the seminary and Manto Fair, there were actually none. He composed a list in his mind and struck each item off quickly; the footbridge, the canal, the dispensary, the little coir factories where they made ropes of varying thickness, the handicraft unit that crafted wild animals out of coconut shells, the little mosque behind which his father was buried; none seemed to fit to the rank of an attraction.

'Alright. Take us to the marshes,' the Mother Superior said. 'The geologist we met on the boat said we should not miss it.'

If the pier was the veranda of the island, the marshes were the scrapyard. People hardly went there, and when they did they went by stealth and pillaged firewood, like his mother did when she ran out of kindling. Why the Bald Blue Shirt qualified it as a must-see, Latif could not understand. Going to the marshes meant walking the entire length of the island and, the worst part, walking past his home. He looked at the houseboat that was still docked, he could bypass his home if they were waterborne.

'It's far away. Let's go on the houseboat,' he said.

'No.' The Mother Superior shook her head. 'This is a walking tour. We will walk.'

And they walked. In little groups that chattered like broken radios. Down the street Latif had once believed to be the busiest place on earth, past places that he had long stopped seeing. He was surprised when a girl turned hysterical at the view of the river through a grove, when another said this was the place she wanted to spend the rest of her life, when one of the Sisters announced she would get a transfer to the seminary if they allowed nuns to teach the novices. He even suspected, that by singing praises of the island, they were being kind to him.

The walking tour had an unscheduled stopover at the footbridge. The girls stopped to admire the canal, then they leaned over the railings and clicked their tongues at the shoals of tiny fishes that zipped downstream as if they were at a zoo and the fish were monkeys. In the morning the water had flowed dark and thick under the footbridge, now it ran clear and fast, rich with burbles, full of parrah barb.

'Enough of this,' said the Mother Superior. 'Let's go to the marshes. And no one stops until our guide does.'

Entering the alley, the girls marvelled at the twists and turns it took and started plucking purple flowers from the fences. He was relieved to see his front yard deserted, but as he passed the house he heard his mother yell at a thieving cat. He imagined his room in a few years from then, and saw Paru lying on his bed, waiting for the blare of the morning boat, thirsting for the touch of his neatly clipped fingers.

The marshes pounced on them with the stench of decomposed coconut husk, and Latif looked apologetically at the excursion.

'Girls, do you recognize the smell?' the leaner of the Sisters asked. 'Can you identify the chemical?'

'Oh no,' moaned the girls in unison.

'Anyone?' she asked. 'You all know the smell. Just name the chemical.'

The girls started to sniff as if collectively grieving for the island, and they shook their heads. One by one, they drifted away to the edge of the marshes.

'What does it smell like to you?' the Sister asked Latif who was the only person looking at her.

To him, it smelled like the island had opened its mouth

and puffed out a strong whiff of bad breath in the face of the visitors. He shook his head and smiled peevishly.

'It smells like hydrogen sulphate,' the Sister said, and walked off.

Left alone, Latif found a seat on the motheaten trunk of a fallen tree, half of which had already been chipped away for firewood, probably by his mother. There was nothing more for him to do, and he started to suspect if they had chosen him as the guide just to pay him for what he had done on the boat. The girls circled around the clumps of mangroves, and the nuns sat a little away from him on a rug of dry leaves, their hands wrapped around their knees. Eavesdropping on them, he understood that they had a change of plans, they were not staying overnight at the seminary, they would take the last boat out to the town and stay at the lodge and leave for their city the next morning. He decided to travel with them, his presence on the boat would make the darkness of the river less intimidating for them.

When the fallen tree swayed, he looked sideways. Paru was sitting next to him. For reasons unknown, he wanted to get up and walk away. 'Can I tell you something?' she asked. He cast a quick glance at the nuns, they were lost in their private little canonical chat. He nodded at the girl.

'You know you look a lot like someone famous,' she said, looking deep into his eyes. 'You look like Brad Pitt when he was younger.'

He thought of Batman. He thought she was poking fun at him.

'You know who Brad Pitt is?'

He looked down at his toes. He had once applied Bismi's nail polish on them. That was long ago, only little specks of red remained on his big toes now, like blood congealed under the toenails.

'This is Brad Pitt.' She showed him the picture of a white handsome man of indeterminable age on her phone. Probably they had the same kind of jaws, beyond that he could not see any similarity. 'The moment I saw you yesterday I thought I had seen you before. Not just me, all of us thought so. And just now I realized it is Brad Pitt you look like.'

'I look like my father,' he said defiantly, though a bit proudly.

'And he looks like Brad Pitt?' she asked, tapping on the picture.

He nodded happily, and she slid off the trunk and faced him. 'But your hairstyle is so Audrey Hepburn.'

He found himself touching the curl on his left ear.

'You know who Audrey Hepburn is?' She fiddled with her phone and turned the screen towards him. He saw the black and white picture of a thin, half smiling lady.

'Does your mother look like her by any chance?'

'No,' he said quickly. The lady held a cigarette and her neckline was low, it showed a bit of cleavage.

He could not decide if a hairstyle so Audrey Hepburn-like was a good thing or not, but it was definitely not something that belonged on a man's head. On their way back to the seminary, Latif felt the curls sitting on his ears like an ignominy. The coconut groves along the way were filled with a pale crimson light, and he saw the sun shining weakly above the treetops. The lamps above the seminary gate had come on, though the parish hall still stood unlit in the distance. The girls hurried down the path that led to the white imposing building, but the nuns lingered by the gate, busily discussing something in whispers, casting occasional glances in his direction. Then the Mother Superior came to him and placed her shivering hand under his chin. 'We are taking the seven-twenty boat back to town. Will you come and see us off?'

His mother was surprised that he had to take the evening boat back to work. The barber was even more surprised when he plunked down on the salon chair and asked for a crew cut and hatchet-shaped whiskers. In the expanse of the mirror that he faced he saw the clock on the wall behind him. He had a lot of time before *Jesus* began the last trip out of the island, still he asked for a quick haircut and no head massage that always came free. The curls fell to his shoulders and lap, and he was ashamed that he had been so assiduously cultivating a hairdo that only women wore, that too in the black and white era.

Minus the curls, he looked faintly like the man Paru had shown him on her phone. He looked at the clock, the hands did not seem to have moved much since he had last looked at it.

'The clock is slow?'

'No,' the barber said. 'It's dead.'

The moment he burst through the swing doors of the salon, he heard *Jesus* hoot.

He ran to the pier. He ran so fast people turned to check if he was being chased. Even before he gained a view of the pier, he knew *Jesus* had left the island. He still ran, he ran faster, and stopped only when he saw the tail lamp of the boat bobbing away.

'You are late by three minutes,' said the Bald Blue Shirt, looking up from his watch. He was standing at the gate of the Camp Office, a steaming cup in his hand. 'I was waiting for you.' He held out a few currencies to him. 'The old nun wanted me to hand you this. Take it.'

He turned around and started to run again. He ran home faster than he had run in a long time, his shadow trailing him like an angry dog.

20

*T*he hairline gap on the roof, where the tiles did not properly align, shone with the new day. He woke up to it only on alternate days, and when sloth kept him in bed he would stare at the wisp of light and think of his father's grave, light streaming in through the chinks between the uneven planks that they had placed on his grave before shovelling dirt onto it. But he knew light would never get into the grave, that the darkness they had buried him in would never escape.

When he knew it was morning and not his day off, he thought of the lodge with a shudder, of the morning boat he had missed; by now he should have finished filling the jugs at the water dispenser and loaded them into the lift. He was not sure why he was still in bed, then slowly the memory of the previous night returned. He had woken in the middle of the night, his body scalding hot and his throat sore, and his mother had sponged him into the small hours and fed him two spoons of a concoction while his sisters stood by like sleepy paramedics. It was the river that had made him sick, he was certain about that. But he did not want his mother to know he had swum in probably the deepest part of the waterbody, shivering with excitement every time he came up for air.

On his lips there was not even a memory of the potion of the night before, but the taste of the river still stuck to the roof his mouth, bland and rubbery, like over-chewed bubble gum. With the windows closed and the door open only a crack, the day had not broken in his room, and the daylight caught him unawares as his mother threw the windows open, even though the needle of light on the roof had warned him it was well past midmorning.

'The manager will yell at me tomorrow,' he moaned when his mother pressed the back of her hand to his forehead. The fever had gone, and he was on the brink of breaking a sweat.

'He will not. I went to Quilon Cashews first thing in the morning and made the owner speak to your manager. Good man. He said it was fine with him.' She offered him a loaf of bread, cut into thick slices, but still held together as a single unit as the baker had withdrawn the knife an inch short of the base. There was a glass of ginger tea to go with it. A loaf of bread had always been the reward for running a fever, but he took the ginger tea as the punishment for inviting illness. The regimen to follow was to dip the reward in hot retribution and masticate it, then to stay in bed until the fever broke.

He nibbled at the moist corner of a slice slowly, waiting for his mother to leave the room so that he could empty the glass through the window and eat the sweet bread dry. Through the open window, he saw a crow land on the banana plant near the well. It shifted crabwise until it was sitting in a square of light on the midrib of a yellowing leaf. It sat still for a long moment, as if stuffed, its black plumes shining in the sun, then it cast an angry look at the house and began to caw, agitated.

'Someone is going to pay us a visit,' his mother said, slipping a hand through the window bars and trying to shoo the crow away. If a crow sat, like this, on a banana leaf and cawed incessantly, she took it as the sign of a guest arriving unannounced, though her predictions rarely proved accurate. The crow stayed impervious to the hand that waved and the mouth that hissed, and his mother rushed down the passage, probably to confront it at close quarters with a stone. Latif tipped over the ginger tea through the window and began to gobble down the bread.

He was tearing the fourth slice off the loaf when he heard someone knock on the front door. The house went quiet for a moment, then buzzed with activities as his sisters scurried around to tidy up the front room before letting his mother open the door. After the groan of the bolt being dragged back, there was a long spell of silence. Latif thought it was the man from the electricity board, who unfailingly turned up exactly when they had no money to spare and handed them a bill, which his mother always judged to be inflated. But he heard a different voice, an unfriendly baritone he seemed to have heard before. Curious, he left the loaf on the table and trudged to the front room.

The interpreter sat on the tattered sofa, looking important and haughty in the absence of his superiors.

'Here he is,' he said when Latif emerged from the sunless passage into the front room. 'But your mother said you are not home.'

'I am home,' he said inanely.

'Yes, I can see that,' he replied. 'I have come to take you to the Camp Office. You are wanted urgently there.' Latif detected a strain of threat in his voice.

'He is unwell,' his mother said. 'That's why he did not go to work today.'

'He doesn't look even mildly unwell to me,' the interpreter said. 'You are healthy enough to walk up to the Camp Office, aren't you?'

'But why is he wanted at your office?' his mother asked.

'That I am not supposed to tell you. Sorry. All I can tell you is he should be at the office today.'

'The poor child hasn't slept a wink last night.' His mother was close to tears.

Smiling shyly, Bismi breezed into the room, bearing a tray on which sat a glass of ginger tea and the best plate in the house. Latif saw slices from the half loaf he had left in his room arranged like petals on the plate, a ring of carrot for a carpel. He was sure the interpreter would wave the refreshment away. But he accepted the tray gratefully and placed it on his lap.

'Get dressed. I will wait for you,' he said as he folded a slice into four and tucked it into his mouth.

'He is still running a fever,' his mother pleaded. 'He won't be able to walk that far.'

The interpreter picked up a second slice and rolled it into the shape of a sausage. He didn't speak until there was nothing left of the roll. 'But it is important that he comes to the office with me.'

'Can he come tomorrow then?'

'Tomorrow is too late. The chief is going on leave from tomorrow. And he won't be back till next month.'

Latif wondered who the chief was, the ecologist who smoked like a chimney or the Bald Blue Shirt who never stopped smiling.

'Then he will come to the office when your chief is back,' his mother said.

'No, the chief insists he see the boy before he goes.'

'For what? Tell us that first.'

He gulped down the ginger tea to clear his throat, and with a finger on his lips he muffled a burp. 'To tell you the truth, sister, I don't know why he is wanted at the office.'

Latif decided to follow the interpreter to the Camp Office and be done with whatever ordeal that awaited him at the bungalow-like building rather than waiting for a few nervous weeks for the chief to return from his sabbatical. 'I will come with you,' he said bravely.

'I will come with you then,' his mother said.

'No,' Latif said sternly. 'I will go alone.'

'You can come, sister. But on one condition. Please don't create a scene like last time.'

'What have you done this time?' Beema muttered when he went inside to change. He didn't remember being a part of any wrongdoing, unless the chief was Georgie's uncle.

He faced the broken mirror as if for a clue and detected unallayed fear in his tired eyes. The white shirt hung in the small almirah, good enough for another wear before washing, but he chose an old tee. With the curls gone, styling his hair was a simple task, a quick swipe of the comb to the right, then to the left. He readied himself slowly and returned to the front room to find the plate empty and the ginger tea drunk to the dregs, and the interpreter picking his teeth with a matchstick.

They walked in silence, struggling to keep up with the quick-footed man. As they crossed the footbridge, his mother whispered to him that she would go to Quilon Cashews and get help if something bad developed at the Camp Office. He glared at his mother, she was making him nervous, she was making him question himself as if he had actually done something wrong.

At the portico of the Camp Office, the interpreter suddenly regained the air of haughtiness he had shed at the sight of refreshment. With an almost angry mime he asked them to wait and then hurried inside as if to compensate for the time he had spent eating the half loaf. He returned immediately and waved them into the office that had once been the home of a congenial old couple.

The chief was neither the ecologist nor the Bald Blue Shirt, but a squat middle-aged man the building had hidden from Latif hitherto. He had a girl's hairstyle; the sides of his head were decorated with the kind of curls Latif had the barber snip away the previous evening. He sat on a swivelling chair with padded armrests, his left foot resting on his right knee, his right foot tapping a slow rhythm on the floor as he took deep drags from a cigarette. Latif thought he looked like a don in distress, someone who was certain to scream the roof down after the initial display of thorough fortitude. On the wall behind the swivelling chair was the photograph of the Anglo-Indian couple, hung with a garland that seemed to have been made by looping wood shavings into a twine, and on the windowsills were the fading stains coffee mugs had left behind as the proof of the dead couple's existence. For a moment Latif wondered if the chief was their runaway son.

'You know what this boy did yesterday?' the chief asked Latif's mother. Latif was surprised that the chief spoke their language, though with a strange accent that made Latif want to mimic him when he was back home.

'I don't know,' his mother confessed. 'He never tells me anything.'

The Bald Blue Shirt came into the room and, finding no vacant chair, sat on the edge of a desk and crossed his hands across his chest.

'He did a brave thing,' the chief said. 'He risked his life to save a boatful of people, including one of my best men.'

His mother studied Latif with unbelieving eyes. He had let her down so many times that she found it hard to believe that the boy was finally worthy of such praise. The tears that rushed to her eyes were real. Even he, the fiercest yet silent critic of her sadness, thought so. 'He is like his father' was all she could manage to say.

'I have heard about his father too,' said the chief, turning in his chair to rub the cigarette out in the pit of an ashtray. He picked up a brown envelope from the table and held it out to Latif, paddling the chair forward with his feet to come nearer to him. 'Take it. This is for you.' A few weeks after his father's death, the ecologist's widow had offered him an envelope that had the same emblem on the front.

'No,' his mother said before he could reach for the envelope. 'We don't want money. He did not do that for money, just like his father.'

The Bald Blue Shirt smiled politely at the mother and son and said something that made the chief smile.

'Just see what's inside,' the chief said. 'If you don't like it, I will take it back.'

His mother took the envelope and opened it carefully as if she expected crisp notes to slide out. There was only a sheet of paper inside. She stared at it briefly before thrusting it into Latif's hands. He stared at it too and gave it back to her.

'You didn't understand anything?' the chief asked.

'No,' they said in unison.

'I thought as much. Let me tell you what the letter says. This boy is going to work with us,' the chief said. And a round of applause erupted like someone had blown out a birthday candle. When it showed no sign of abating, Latif dreaded his mother would join in and outdo the others.

'It is a temporary job, of course,' the chief said when the office finally fell quiet. 'But we will renew the contract every year as long as this office stands. I am sure this setup will be around long enough to see this boy getting married and starting his family.'

Latif heard *Jesus* pull in, wailing, and saw commuters stroll past the Camp Office, unaware of what was happening in his life.

'It's a nine to five job,' the chief said. 'You will dust and clean the office, run errands, collect mail, make tea for us and collect the dispatches the boat brings from the mainland. It is not a very difficult job.'

It sounded nothing short of a dream job to Latif. He could picture himself entering the Camp Office at nine in the morning and leaving at five. He could picture himself getting married, watched by his colleagues, rearing children, pampered by his sisters, and watching his own TV, surrounded by his family.

'He will come at nine tomorrow, sir,' his mother said.

'Not tomorrow,' the chief chuckled. 'He can join next week. There is some paperwork to be done. That man over there will help you do that.' He pointed to a clerk who cracked a smile at the boy and the mother and summoned them to his desk.

'If he makes a mistake, punish him the way you like,' his mother said as the chief got up from the chair. 'Nobody will ask.'

The paperwork took longer than Latif had expected, he was made to fill many forms and sign several declarations, and each word he wrote made him happier, made him hate the lodge more and more. The office emptied as the evening wore on until there were only Latif, his mother and the clerk left in the room. The last boat had already left the island when Latif finished signing the documents and got up to go home.

They were so happy that they fought all the way home. They fought over the week ahead, and they fought like siblings. His mother started it, she wanted him to stay at home for what remained of the week and convalesce. He wanted to take one last trip to the town and bid a proper goodbye to the lodge. She insisted he resign over the phone, just a call from Quilon Cashews would do. He stood firm about taking the morning boat to work, he wanted to collect the dues and say goodbyes. She said she was not going to get up early in the morning to cook him another lunch. He thanked her profusely for that, he never really enjoyed those cold lunches, he would go to a small eatery near the jetty and buy himself lunch. She pulled a face, and he pulled a face too, and they walked in silence, and both hid their smiles knowing that they had never fought so good-naturedly before.

'Why do you keep looking back?' she asked when they entered the dark street that led to the footbridge. 'Is something wrong?'

It was only then did he realize that he had been looking over his shoulder every now and then since they left the Camp Office. He was checking if Georgie was following them. His life could not have taken a better turn, and it was the perfect night for Georgie to return to the island and stick a knife into his back. Those tragic movies he had watched could not have been founded on mere fiction.

'Nothing,' he said. 'Walk faster. The girls are waiting.'

21

The wind from the river rustled the shabby see-through curtains of the small hotel that sat on the far side of the jetty, made of timber and tin, its back turned to the town. From where he sat, Latif could see the grimmer side of the dredger, white and green and the deep brown of corrosion. He absently marvelled at the way the creepers skirted the big patch of rust and climbed to the roof. When a teacher had told his class that plants had life and could breathe like humans, he had secretly laughed at the unconvincing lie, but now he started to think how carefully the creepers steered clear of the rust, taking cautious strides with its little clumps of roots around the vast pool of frozen brownness.

It was that hour of the day when the jetty wore the look of something long abandoned, like the dredger, a thing left to rot and dust. No boats, no commuters, not even a stray dog, the shutter down on the ticket booth and the clerk nowhere in sight.

Stella ate slowly, eyeing the river blankly. A cloud of sadness had passed over her face when he told her that morning that it was his last day at the lodge, the last day in the town that he had not had the courage to explore beyond the roundabout. She touched him lightly on the shoulder and said she was happy that he had landed a proper job so early in life. Now, as they sat across the narrow wooden table, she looked sad again. He did not know what to tell her, he had never bidden farewell to anyone before. He thought of telling her a lunchtime story for the last time, but the tale of Ibru being rewarded for his bravery was nothing new, Ibru had already been rewarded enough times. In fact, Latif had long been thinking about expelling Ibru from the lunchbreak chats. He had been finding it difficult to invent new adventures for his alter ego, and Stella's knowing smile had slowly turned into a sneer. He wondered if it would be a good idea to tell her about the chores that the chief had listed out for him. But it would only make the new job look many shades inferior to that of a bellboy. So he pecked at the lunch in silence.

In the morning, the manager had received the news of his leaving with such nonchalance that Latif regretted not following his mother's advice and calling the lodge from Quilon Cashews and hanging up on the manager after curtly telling him why he had called. To lessen the hurt he went from floor to floor, door to door, and bade farewell to the permanent lodgers. Some feigned shock, some smiled at him for the first time, some slipped money into his hand. By noon, he was moneyed enough to buy Stella lunch from one of the better eateries up the street. But she insisted they go to the small one near the jetty where coolies and hawkers lunched.

'New shirt?' she asked, fixing her glance on a red button.

'Yes, my mother bought me this for my birthday.'

It was the first time he was wearing the white shirt to work. It had been neither washed nor worn since the day he had walked the excursion through the island, and it smelled faintly of sweat under the armpits (and he thought it smelled of the marshes as well) but he had chosen to wear it to elongate the sense of accomplishment that had overwhelmed him when he signed document after document at the Camp Office.

'Aren't you inviting me home?' she asked, finishing the lunch.

He fumbled for words for a while, then blurted out, 'You should come to our village one day. There are lots of places to see. You can take the morning boat to the island and evening boat back. I will show you around.'

'But you are still not inviting me home?'

'Yes, yes,' he said quickly. 'You should come home.'

'I will,' she said. 'I will pay you a surprise visit.'

He dreaded she would one day honour her promise and land on the island. It would be easy for her to find his home, she would only need to ask the women who worked at Quilon Cashews and one of them would happily give her directions, even accompany her to his home if she was free, while he would be busy making tea at the Camp Office or dusting the photograph of the Anglo-Indian couple. But his immediate concern was not about her visit, but about Stella footing the bill for lunch. That would have hurt his pride, and he kept miming to the waiter to bring the bill to him when she was staring vacantly at the river. Stella did not snatch the bill when it was brought to their table on a little saucer, anchored with cumin seeds; she watched him pay with a smile shining in her eyes, and then they left the eatery and rounded the jetty building to the main street.

They were passing the straggling line of shops when she suddenly grabbed him by the wrist and dragged him into a footwear store. 'Let me buy you a small present,' she said. He crimsoned, he wanted to protest, to run away, to decline, but he meekly followed her into the shop, longing for a gift. The shop was poky and dimly lit, and for a moment he thought the shop assistant who sprang to his feet was Georgie, he was as young and lanky as Latif's schooltime rival—he even had an unfriendly face studded with pimples. But he was not Georgie.

Stella led him to the rack arrayed with shoes and asked him to pick anything he liked. His eyes fell on a pair of red sports shoes and lingered there long enough for her to ask the shop assistant if they were the right size for Latif. They fit snugly onto his small feet, and he paced the length of the shop in the fake Nike to ensure that they did not pinch him on the move. When she paid for the shoes, he looked away, and felt an urge to buy her something from the next shop, a brooch or a pair of cheap earrings. But the urge did not last, and they soldiered past the shops to the lodge.

Latif remembered a farewell party from a long time ago. He vividly remembered the afternoon; the entire school had waited in the quad while the teachers sat around the retiring headmaster in the staff room and stuffed themselves with patties and plantains. The children were later asked to line up for a photo session under the gooseberry trees, and Latif, owing to his small build, earned a place in the first row, sitting lopsided on the floor at the feet of the outgoing teacher. In the years that followed, every time he passed the staff room, he stole a glance at the photograph hanging next to the world map like a certificate of merit.

As the evening approached, he longed for a photo session under the gulmohar, surrounded by the staff and the inmates of Paradise Lodge; a copy of the photograph would hang in the lobby and another next to his father's picture as the proof of his first job, the relic of the time he had spent on the mainland. But when the sky turned to a deep ash, he knew there would be no photo. The walls of the lobby were bereft of pictures, and he was sure that many bellboys had worked in the lodge and quit, and none of them had been given a send-off. He was not special, he was just being too ambitious, prompted by Stella's gift. As there was nothing else to do, he opened the box and pulled on the red shoes and started to walk up and down the lobby with his eyes lowered to the ground, as if looking for dropped coins.

When Stella came to the lobby to say goodbye, he was still making his feet friendly with the shoes. She looked at his feet and smiled, and he simply blushed. He felt like a child who started to eat the savouries a guest had brought, only to find that the guest had not actually left the house.

'Don't forget us,' she said in an almost broken voice, pointing to the phone on the counter. 'Call me whenever you have time.'

He feared she would plant a kiss on his forehead, but she merely gave him a pat on his head and turned to leave. She stopped when the drone of an engine wafted into the lobby. They stooped a little to look through the window, their heads juxtaposed, and saw a police jeep roll into the forecourt and stop under the gulmohar.

'What now?' Stella asked, frowning mildly.

A car drove in through the gate, moving slowly as if it had lost its way, and stopped behind the jeep. Latif saw the dead actor, the rightful owner of the shirt he was wearing, step out of the car and walk towards the lobby.

22

'*A*re you out of your mind?' Stella asked the nervous boy, smiling. But there was something uncertain about her smile that told him she was as discomfited as himself. 'How can he be the dead actor? This man is his brother. His twin brother. He is a singer or a musician. I am not sure which.'

A knot loosened at his chest, but a trembling coldness remained somewhere in the pit of his stomach as if he had accidentally swallowed an ice cube or two. He watched the dead actor's brother and three policemen stand with their elbows on the counter talking to the manager with forced civility, as if they were trying to negotiate on the tariff. The manager spoke politely, unsmiling, his right hand repeatedly going up to check his Adam's apple. Latif peered past the men at the clock, it was a quarter to six. In fifteen minutes, the last boat would leave the town, and an hour later, it would dock at the dark pier. He had planned to take the morning boat, like he did on every second day but, as on his first day as a bellboy, he now wanted to be home before he was expected. If he took the boat, he would be home in time for supper. Though he was not even remotely hungry, he longed for a homecooked dinner and the rough warmth of his narrow bed.

'Why are they here?' he mumbled to Stella, who was studying the men curiously as if they had stepped into the lobby straight out of a story book.

'I don't know,' she said absently. 'Maybe they are just completing some formality.'

'I am going home,' he said, turning around in his new shoes. 'Will you tell the manager that I have left?'

'Are you mad?' she whispered, her eyes still fixed on the men, her head cocked at an angle in her effort to eavesdrop on them. 'You are leaving without taking the dues? It is your money, idiot. And I thought you said you were taking only the morning boat.'

'My mother asked me to be home for supper.'

They heard another police jeep arrive; it drove past the gulmohar and came to a stop so close to the windows that the headlights turned the panes yellow and magnified the grey mottles on them. The engine ran for a while, thrumming angrily, then died down, and the windows turned dark, the mottles invisible. Speaking quietly on the phone, an inspector walked in, and the constables stiffened in his presence. The man's uniform was a darker khaki than that of his subordinates and his face was so handsome Latif took him for an actor, and, in the light of this new judgement, he took the constables for supporting cast. All of a sudden, he was almost certain why they had come to the lodge. They must be enacting the last day of the dead actor for a documentary film, and he thought the twin brother playing the dead brother was a masterstroke. Only the police jeeps left him disconcerted, probably they too were just dressed up to look like real ones.

The life on the island had never afforded him a chance to watch a movie being filmed, and now that it was about to happen right in front of his eyes he was ready to leave the town for good. The crew should have come a week earlier, or he should have decided to stay back for a few more days. As he watched the inspector talk to the manager, he was intrigued about the way they would portray the scene in which the actor's body was discovered. He could envision a man opening the door and stepping into the half dark room, a boy standing behind him. In his mental picture, the boy was much younger than him, he did not know why, but he thought young boys were cut out to suffer a lot in movies. Who would play the manager? The manager himself? Who would play the bellboy? He?

'Are they going to shoot a movie here?' he whispered

to Stella.

'What?' she asked, looking surprised. 'A movie? What makes you think so?'

He could not think up an answer. The knot at his chest tightened again at the possibility of the policemen and their jeeps being real.

'It's not a movie. I think the manager is in real trouble,' Stella said, more to herself than to him.

The manager picked up the key from the hook that had 555 written under it and followed the men into the lift. Latif remembered the Mexican footballer being shown a red card and sent off the pitch. 'Mind the counter,' he told Stella as he passed them. 'I won't be long.'

'He is in trouble?' Latif asked Stella as they sat on the bench and listened to the lift clanging up the shaft. 'Why is he in trouble?'

'Don't ask me why. But I think he is in trouble.' The lift stopped on the fifth floor, and they heard the pulleys strain and shiver. The shutters banged shut and then there was only silence down the dark shaft.

It had barely been half an hour since sunset. But the darkness under the gulmohar had the depth of midnight. Latif stretched his legs into the radius of the light falling from the bulb suspended above the counter and sized up his shoes critically, as if he was yet to buy them. He began to notice the minute details that he had missed earlier in the evening—the way the soles curved in and culminated in a triangle at the toes, the intertwining shades of the lace, the shape of the eyelets and the red swoosh on the white tongue. Stella picked up an old newspaper from behind the water dispenser and, tearing a sheet into two, started to model a plane from it.

As they waited for the manager to return, thin bolts of lightning appeared behind the distant treeline and the skies started to rumble. In spite of the light and sound, the air was muggy, but Latif was certain that deep down the river it had started to rain, soaking the archipelago as the monsoon coasted towards the mainland. On rainy nights, he moved his bed to the centre of the room because the hairline gap between the rooftiles leaked onto the headboard. If it rained on the island, he would return home to find the pillow drenched, as if a girl—a nameless, faceless virgin—had wept for him, heartbroken by his absence.

The clock struck eight, then nine, and the hands of the old Seiko appeared to be as fatigued as Stella, as bored as Latif. They were startled by the grunt of the intercom. Stella dropped the paper plane to the floor but did not get up from the bench, and finally it was Latif who answered it.

'Who is Stella?' a man's voice asked.

'She is here,' he said, turning to face her and summon her to the counter.

'Who is Latif?' the man's voice asked before he could offer the phone to Stella.

'I am Latif,' he stuttered.

'Come to Room No. 555. Both of you,' the voice said, and the line went dead.

The ride to the fifth floor was the slowest he had ever taken in his stint as a bellboy, and also the noisiest, the metallic thuds echoing like church bells as they went past landing after dark landing, and even though he was not burdened with laundry or water jugs, he felt his hands were unbearably heavy. When the lift jerked to a stop, they walked reluctantly out and stumbled down the corridor like sleepwalkers.

A constable was waiting for them outside Room No. 555, as if they stood a chance of losing their way in the dark corridor otherwise. When they stepped into the room, Latif heard the door close quietly behind them. All the lights were shining, even the reading lamp near the bed, and they appeared to have entered a strange place where the shadows had been folded neatly and stowed away in the cupboard. The inspector and the dead actor's brother sat on the bed, and the constables stood by the window, hiding the view of the gulmohar. The manager occupied the only chair in the room, his hands placed between his knees, fingers interlocked. Latif looked at his hands to see if they were in cuffs, but they were free, if anything they were just nervous.

'I just want to ask you some questions,' the inspector said. His voice was as kind as his face was handsome. 'It won't take long. We all have homes to go back to, don't we? It is already late.'

The inspector wore shiny beige shoes, and white specks of light shone on their tips. Latif raised his eyes from them to find that the inspector was studying his red sport shoes with interest. 'My first question is who found the body in this room,' he asked.

'I did, sir,' the manager said. His voice had gone papery.

'No,' the inspector said. 'I am asking these two. I want answers from them.'

'The manager did, sir,' Stella said.

'Was he alone when the body was discovered?'

'No,' Latif said. 'I was with him.'

'Good.' The inspector smiled at Latif. 'Now my questions are open to all three of you.'

Latif readied himself to answer first, at school he never had answers, and customarily winced when questions were directed at him.

'Was anybody alone with the body at any point in time before the police arrived?'

Latif held his tongue, that was not the question he

had anticipated. He looked at the manager, who tilted his head to the side in a pretence of remembering the evening. 'Yes, when I went to the lobby to inform the police, Latif was here in the room. He was alone,' the manager said.

'Did you ask him to stay back?' the inspector asked.

'No, sir,' the manager said. 'I thought he was following me and only when I got into the lift did I realize that he was not with me.'

'Interesting,' the inspector said, looking at Latif. 'How old are you?'

'I am eighteen,' he said, almost proudly.

'Are you sure? You don't look even sixteen to me.'

'Yes, my eighteenth birthday was four months ago.'

'Well, that is a relief.' The inspector turned to address the constables. 'We don't need to involve a juvenile welfare body for this.' The constables nodded in polite agreement.

Latif did not understand what the inspector said. He waited for the next question, he only wished it was a simple one.

'Someone bring a chair for him,' the inspector said. 'How long should we keep him standing?' Latif liked the way the inspector conducted himself, he was polite, smiling and, in spite of his eagerness to go home, patient.

A constable brought a chair from the passage and placed it behind Latif. The constable did not look as friendly as the inspector, he had a bloated pockmarked face and the eyes of a drunkard. Latif sat down and assumed the same posture as the manager, leaning forward, fingers interlocked and hands placed between the knees.

'Now, Latif, tell me just one thing. Then we all can go home.'

He thought of cracking a joke about the bench in the lobby being his home for the night, that he was taking only the early morning boat to the island, that he had all the time in the world to answer the questions. He could imagine the room erupting into laughter. But he merely nodded at the inspector.

'Where is that ring you removed from the dead body? We would not have come for it after all these months had it not been six sovereigns plus some precious stones. And the family attaches some sentimental value to it and wants it back.'

Latif felt the eyes of the actor's brother boring into his skull, and the pain it created was almost palpable. 'I don't know anything about the ring,' he said.

'Of course you do,' the inspector said. 'Probably you didn't remove it from the body, you must have found it lying around and thought of keeping it. I can understand that.'

214

'No, I didn't take the ring,' he said and, as if to prove his innocence, pressed a hand to where the pocket had been. 'I took only this shirt from the room.'

'But you said your mother bought this as a birthday gift,' Stella said, and she stopped abruptly as if she had said something wrong. It surprised him that she was still in the room. He had not looked in her direction since he had been offered the chair.

'Does this shirt belong to your brother?' the inspector asked the actor's brother.

'He had a white shirt. But I am not sure if it is the same one. His shirt never had red buttons.'

'It had white buttons,' Latif reassured the brother, he was almost out of breath from excitement. 'I lost them in a fight.'

'Whom did you fight with?' the inspector asked. He sounded amused, eager to listen to stories of fistfights in faraway lands.

'Georgie,' he said. 'He was my classmate.'

'You fought over the ring?' the inspector asked. 'Or the money you got from selling it?'

'No, he and his friends tried to beat me up because I once stabbed him with a pencil.'

A hush fell over the room and Latif heard the skies rumble again, closer this time, directly above the lodge.

He closed his eyes for a moment and he saw the pier, it was empty, *Jesus* had collected the last batch of commuters and left for the town, it was pouring with rain on the island, the wind from the river sweeping the dirt on Manto Road to the sidewalk.

'Feeling sleepy?' He heard the inspector's voice and opened his eyes.

'No,' he said.

'Want a cigarette or something to freshen you up?'

'He doesn't smoke,' said Stella in a voice laced with helpless anger.

'I smoked only once,' he said.

'Really? I used to smoke a lot,' the inspector said. 'Then I quit. I haven't touched a cigarette in five years. But you smoked just one cigarette and quit? That's great. You didn't like the taste a bit?'

Latif realized that something strange had come over him. Every time the inspector asked him a question he remembered something from his island, a road, a building, a fallen tree serving as a bridge over a ditch. He now remembered the marshes, the view of the river through the mangroves. 'I smoked because he beat me up,' he pointed a finger at the manager, expecting him to protest or even to deny having ever so much as pinched him. But the accusation made the manager look only relaxed, which angered Latif. 'He beat me with a mop.'

The smile waned from the inspector's face, and he looked murderously at the manger. 'Did you beat this little boy? And that too with a mop?'

'Yes, sir, I did, because he peeped into a guest's room when...,' he stopped and grinned.

'Latif, did you peep into a room when the guests were...,' the inspector also stopped mid-sentence and grinned. Latif thought he was mimicking the manager.

He did not know how to answer that question without provoking laughter from the people around him. He closed his eyes and saw a house he used to walk past on his way to school. It stood at a bend in a narrow road, it had potted hydrangeas hanging from the awning; the flowers, blue and purple, never looked real, they seemed to have come off the shelf, they were never meant to wilt.

'Did you or did you not?' the inspector asked.

'I did,' he said, opening his eyes.

They heard the manager clear his throat, as if asking for permission to speak. 'Sir, I think he is lying about smoking only once. I have seen him quite a few times standing under the star fruit tree behind the office and smoking.'

For the first time since he had staked the pencil into the deodar in the fairground, Latif felt up to screaming. Screaming and screaming until someone gagged him. He swallowed the scream, it tasted like unripe tamarind.

'I am not interested in his smoking habits,' the inspector said crossly.

'Just a minute, sir,' the manager said. 'I just remembered something. I don't know if it means anything. But one night I saw him digging a hole under the star fruit tree.'

Latif saw heads turn, faces brighten, and bodies go slack with relief.

'Did you hide the ring in a hole?' The inspector got up from the bed and arched his back.

Latif now saw the seminary building and the back of the Virgin Mary's statue. There was a thin film of moss on the folds of her concrete robe. 'No, I never dug a hole under the tree.'

'That is what we are going to find out now,' the inspector said and walked to the door. Latif felt a hand on his shoulder and turned his head to see the constable with the pockmarked face standing behind him, gesturing at him to get up.

'Let's start digging again,' he said, wrapping a hand around Latif's shoulders and leading him down the dark corridor which looked, at least to him, darker than ever before.

23

*U*nder the bright beams of several torches, the fallen leaves resembled faces of withered old men, veiny and grievous. It was silent under the star fruit tree, except for the scrapings that lathis made on the dry ground as the constables swept the windfalls aside in search of loose earth. Stella was in the pantry, looking for a hoe, and he heard the inspector ask what was taking her long. Latif imagined her slipping behind the counter to make a quick call to Quilon Cashews, instructing the owner to send his mother to the lodge by the first boat. Then he remembered that she did not know the phone number of Quilon Cashews, she did not even know it existed.

A torch swung up from the ground and shone on his face, and he clamped his eyes shut and turned his profile to the beam, unintentionally grinding his teeth. He was growing as impatient as the inspector. Once the hoe arrived, holes sank and nothing but earthworms excavated, his ordeal would be over, he would most certainly be apologised to, the manager would be interrogated again, and the inspector would finally lose his head. The prospect of the night being long and dramatic filled him with an edgy enthusiasm. The last time he experienced something remotely similar was on the night before Uncle Koya's son got married, when he stayed awake till sunrise staking fern leaves into the thatched walls of the wedding venue. He saw the arrangement of the leaves now, rows of fluffy green that gradually turned to copper and fell off. The light swung away from his face, and he opened his eyes again.

Stella came out through the back door of the lobby and walked unhurriedly towards the little huddle of men under the star fruit tree. A hoe dangled from her left hand, like something that could untangle Latif's life with a few swings through the mould.

'Why did you take so long?' the inspector asked.

'I had to make a call,' she said. It was then Latif remembered that the phonebook in the lobby had the number of Quilon Cashews, written alongside his name.

'Did you make a call? Whom did you call?' The inspector's voice was hard.

'I called home. I told them I would be late.' Latif's heart sank.

'Nobody will make calls without asking me first. Understand?' The inspector sounded like someone older now, someone with an ugly face and a paunch. 'Give the hoe to the boy.'

When he took the hoe from Stella, Latif gave her a half wink, reassuring her that he would come clean, it was just a matter of minutes before things started to work in his favour, and it would be a happy ending for everyone except the manager. But he was not sure if she had noticed him wink, it was just a half wink, and it was half dark under the tree.

'Start now,' the inspector said. 'I hope you remember where you have dug last time.'

Where the hoe made the first contact with the earth, the light from the torches made a floral pattern, one petal of shivering glow stitched to another until they made a rough circle on the coffee brown dirt. He worked earnestly, as if he was going to be paid for the job, grunting softly every time the blade sliced the ground. He dragged the loose earth up and heaped them around the emerging pit like oversized anthills and, when the hole was big enough to trap a foot, he paused and looked up, convinced that his innocence had been proven.

'You don't remember the exact position?' the inspector asked. 'Try a new place.'

The beams moved to a new spot, and he started to work the hoe on the ground again. Slowly his face turned wet, and nobody could tell if it was sweat or tears that rolled down his cheeks, not even himself. All he knew was it was not raindrops. The skies still rumbled faintly, and lightning occasionally flashed behind distant trees. A star fruit fell to his feet with a soft thud, and he turned it into pulp under his new shoes. When the second hole grew bigger than the first and turned out to be as empty, he moved to a new spot, without even being told, and the rings of light obediently followed his movement.

Half-way through the fifth hole he started to wonder what his mother and sisters would be doing at that very moment; they must be in bed by now, a little sleepier every time the hoe hit the ground.

'Stop.' He heard the inspector behind him. 'Are you sure you saw him digging a hole?'

'Yes, sir, I saw him digging a hole,' the manager said. His voice was laboured, as if he was the one who had been forced to till in the middle of the night.

'Where were you when you saw him?'

'I was standing there.' The manager pointed to a lit window of the lobby. Latif saw the edge of the water dispenser in the corner of a pane, the rest of the window was filled with a stretch of bare wall. The bareness of the pale blue wall pricked a sharp pain in his chest.

'He was standing on this side of the tree or the other side when you saw him?'

ANEES SALIM

'I am not sure.' There was a brief spell of silence. 'I think he was standing on the other side.'

The beams moved to the far side of the tree, and Latif followed the trail of light, the fallen fruits popping out under the weight of his fatigue. The series of holes he had dug had made a narrow trench around the tree, except for a short strip which awaited the touch of the hoe.

'Try to remember,' the inspector said, a finger directed at a tuff of flowering carnations. 'Is this where you hid the ring?'

Latif saw the footbridge, the canal gushing under it, he saw the big rock which divided the flow, he saw a crane land on it to rest and then, unsettled by a slingshot, swoop through a silent estate towards the river.

'Don't say you don't know,' the inspector said darkly. 'Go on, dig.'

The sound the hoe made on the earth had a crisp twang to it, like the beat of a folksong. He listened to the refrain, he was determined not to upset its cadence. His grunts had acquired a baritone, and he was starting to believe that it came from someone else, probably from the constable with the pockmarked face as a way of prompting him. The hoe made a ding inside the pit and its blade caught something. Latif spooned a muddy bundle to the foot of the tree, and the circles of light hungrily closed in on it. It was a small cylinder wrapped in a piece of cloth, secured with a jute string.

'Open it,' the inspector demanded.

Latif went down to his knees as if in prayer, and slowly undid the jute string, then he removed the cloth wrapper, revealing an old can of baby food.

'Open the lid,' the inspector said softly.

Latif prised open the lid and peered inside, the light from the torches highlighted the powdery rust that had collected along the rim of the can. For a moment he thought the can was empty, then he saw a small screw of newspaper lying at the bottom. He reached for it with a hand that had grown numb from holding the hoe and lifted it with two fingers as if he was dealing with a dead dragonfly.

A constable spread a handkerchief on the muck and Latif placed the paper screw at the centre of it.

'Open it,' said the inspector.

He pulled the crinkled edges apart and the paper screw fell open like a flower, and there lay the ring, its gems shining weakly in the light from the torches. A hand picked up the ring and, one by one, the orbs of light left the scrap of newspaper. In the sole beam that kept shining on the paper, he read the headline. *Saffron Sweeps Nation.*

'Let's go now,' the inspector said.

Latif heard birds twitter in the trees that flanked the backwall. The dawn could not be far away. Grey crumbs of the sky were already showing through the branches of the star fruit tree. He handed the hoe to Stella and followed the policemen up the footpath that rounded the lobby and led to the forecourt.

The seat of the jeep was cold, he felt the clamminess filter through his trousers and sting the underside of his thighs. His teeth clattered in a sudden gust of breeze from the river, and he hugged himself for comfort, as if his body belonged to someone else.

The headlights filled the windows of the lobby with yellow light, and Stella appeared behind it. She stood still, she looked like a picture. As the jeep rolled backwards, the light on the windows paled and she grew indistinct, and then, lit only by the light in the lobby, she appeared to be standing in a swath of mist.

As the jeep slid out of the compound, a silent drizzle started. The first light of the day hurt his eyes, and he shut them tight. He saw the little letterbox his father had strung to their gate, into which beetles sometimes mailed themselves.

Epilogue

On a cloudy Sunday, Stella took the afternoon boat to Manto Island. The boat was late to dock and the jetty was almost empty. She went to the small eatery behind the weatherworn jetty office and sat at the same table where they had eaten on Latif's last day at work, staring through the see-through curtains. The horn of the incoming boat sounded like a warning for her to turn back and go home. But she persisted.

Until she reached the end of the short gangplank, she did not know that a boat named *Jesus* existed. And the picture of Jesus above the door to the driver's cabin calmed her nerves, assured her that no turbulence awaited her on the waters.

Soon after the town disappeared from sight, the sky brightened and the sun deepened the jade of the river. The journey, like every first journey, looked longer than it actually was, and every time the boat passed an island she readied herself to disembark. Finally, forty minutes later, the boat slowed down and showed the signs of going ashore. From the distance, Manto Island looked like a crocodile, and she wondered from which angle did it resemble a bra.

The pier was as deserted as the jetty. Getting off the boat, the silence of the island surprised her, and she wondered for a moment if she had been accidentally dropped off at an uninhabited island. She walked nervously down the worn path until she spotted a tottering building with pockmarked walls as if it had recently faced a firing squad. A tin board with flaking paint hung on the doorway, reading *Quilon Cashews*. Behind the building was a shed where a row of women sat on their haunches, shelling cashews. She asked the first woman in the row for the directions to Pir Muhammed's house. For some strange reason, she did not want to take Latif's name. The woman stopped working and looked kindly, almost gratefully, at her, as if giving directions gave her the much-needed reprieve. Picking up a knife, she drew a route map on the red earth. The twisting and turning lines the knife carved on the floor confused Stella; after a point, they seemed to confuse the lady herself. She hauled herself to her feet and shouted to a boy who was pedalling by, 'Take this aunty to Mandrake's house.'

'I am not going in that direction,' the boy shouted back.

'She is from the town. She doesn't know the way. Help her.'

'I don't have time. I have a football match.'

'Okay. Come home after your match. You won't get a thing to eat. You can boil and have the football for supper.'

The boy, who was roughly Latif's age, stamped his barefoot on the ground in exasperation. Then he grudged Stella a smile and invited her to sit on the carrier behind the seat. She refused, even after the lady reminded her that Mandrake's house was nearly a kilometre away. She promised the boy to follow his bicycle on foot as fast as her tired legs would allow her. The boy was displeased at the prospect of doing a solo slow race across the island. But he complied.

The boy and his bicycle did a graceless waltz up Manto Road, the handle of his bicycle trembling and twisting in the sluggish pace he forced, down a warren of narrow lanes, across a footbridge and many footpaths, past a straggling row of hideous houses and finally down an alley fenced by flowering quickstick plants before stopping in front of a little wooden gate covered with creepers. A small house stood at the end of a short drive carpeted with dry leaves; it seemed to have been abandoned for a while. The creepers that had climbed up the latticed windows were just weeks away from conquering the roof.

'Are you sure this is the house?'

'Yes, this is the house,' the boy said, turning the bicycle around to head out of the alley. 'It was my father who found the bodies first. He found the lady's body in the front room and the girls in the bedroom.'

She found it hard to peel her eyes off the crumbling house, and it took the boy to tinkle the bell busily to attract her attention. 'It is easy to find your way back. In case you get lost, just ask anyone.'

The boy mounted the bicycle and arched his back for the ride back.

'By the way, do you know a boy named Ibru?'

'Yes, I know. He is in jail now.' He looked over his shoulder and then pedalled away.

Stella did not ask him to stop, she knew the way back to the pier. She stood listening to the birds chirp in the unruly garden behind the wooden gate, she watched a squirrel scurry across the roof. As she turned the corner to leave, she paused to look at the alley behind her. Empty and straight, fringed with green leaves and purple flowers, it looked like a path one walked only in dreams.

Acknowledgements

Omanakuttan, for listening intently to my stories.

Ambi Parameswaran, for the unconditional love and support.

Abdullah Khan, for his candid evaluation of the manuscript.

Kanishka Gupta, for finding the right home for this book.

Robert Peett, for his faith in this book.

Jo Dalton, for the beautiful cover.

Poppy Britcher, for her patience, support and camaraderie.

Anees Salim

At the age of sixteen, Anees dropped out of school and left home to become a writer. He travelled across India and worked as a bellboy, waiter, shop assistant and ghost writer before joining advertising. He currently works as a Creative Director with FCB India. His published works include *Vanity Bagh* (winner of The Hindu Literary Prize for Best Fiction 2013), *The Blind Lady's Descendants* (winner of the Raymond Crossword Book Award for Best Fiction 2014 and the Kendra Sahitya Akademi Award 2018), *The Small-town Sea* (winner of the Atta Galatta-Banaglore Literature Festival Book Prize for Best Fiction 2017), and *The Odd Book of Baby Names*. His works have been translated into French, German and several Indian languages.

Praises for Anees Salim

'One of the outstanding storytellers in contemporary Indian writing.'
Forbes India

'There's no other way to put it: Anees Salim [...] is one of the most affecting writers working today. As prodigiously talented as he is, he is distinguished from contemporaries writing in English by his precision in identifying and then mining the deep fatalism that runs through the Indian psyche'.
Mint Lounge

'Salim creates a detailed world for his protagonists, delving into their interior lives, looking back to look in. Memory is the leitmotif that runs through all his novels, a thread that binds the past and the future; the present is only as long as one inhabits it.'
Indian Express

'When you read Anees Salim, the sense of time takes leave of you as the author sets about using his pen like a brush to etch out characters who are often at peace with the world but at war with themselves. Some mistake their disappointments for sorrow. Angst is indeed an abiding emotion in his works. Yet, it is seldom depressing. Melancholy is what stays with you as you cover his literary landscape. In fact, his pen transmits the joy of being sad.'
Frontline

'Anees Salim finds big-city success with his satirical small-town stories. [His] literary voice could have gone unheard if not for his dogged persistence, unique talent, and, of course, a bit of luck.'
Caravan

'Salim has created a world veiled with subtle emotion.'
Hindustan Times

'Like an epic author he just looks at the events with a detached gaze that turns even tragedies and crises into just passing scenes from life's comic theatre.'
Frontline

'At some point in our lives, we have to be touched by sadness, and I want to be touched by a sadness that is Anees Salimesque (if I could invent a term like this). There should be beauty and humour in my sadness.'
Scroll

'Salim is a chronicler of the neglected and obscure. The mofussils inhabited by his characters are fenced-in localities of delicate foliage, insignificant landmarks, small triumphs and tragedies.'
The Wire

'He draws his protagonists' worlds in minute detail, digging deep into their inner lives with so much tenderness that the mundane observation often transcends into the memorable. His ability to look at the events from a great distance imbues his writing with a sense of detachment and foreboding, and his players are seen careering towards unfailing tragedy not like a signal-free train, but gently, like an undulating leaf that will silently, but surely, hit the ground.'
Financial Expre

Helen E. Mundler

Three Days by the Sea

*No-one talks about Susie but no-one can forget
her – until Gina and Robert receive invitations to
a family reunion by the sea in Cornwall.*

As the three days unfold, the stories and secrets
of each character are mapped against England's
changing society through the history of the family.
Gradually, the truth of Susie's disappearance over
twenty years ago is revealed as the secrets, griefs,
and eccentricities of one family are exposed to the
Cornish light.

Three Days by the Sea is a subtle, funny and moving
story of hope and renewal. With dry, sharp humour
and warmth, Helen Mundler unpicks the trials and
tensions of family life.

Publication: **19th May 2022**

(Hardcover) ISBN: 978-1-910688-69-4

Ashutosh Bhardwaj

The Death Script:
Dreams and Delusions in Naxal Country

A haunting ode to those who paid the ultimate price—through the prism of the Maoist insurgency, Ashutosh Bhardwaj meditates on larger questions of violence and betrayal, love and obsession, and what it means to live with and write about death.

From 2011 to 2015, Ashutosh lived in the Red Corridor in India wherein the Ultra-Left Naxalites, taking inspiration from the Russian revolution and Mao's tactics, work to overthrow the Indian government by the barrel of the gun. He made several trips thereafter reporting on the insurgents, on police and governmental atrocities, and on the lives caught in the crossfire. *The Death Script* chronicles his experiences and bears witness to the lives and deaths of the unforgettable men and women he meets from both sides of the struggle, bringing home the human cost of conflict with astonishing power. Narrated in multiple voices, the book is a creative biography of the region, Dandakaranya, that combines the rigour of journalism, the intimacy of a diary, the musings of a travelogue, and the craft of a novel.

The Death Script is one of the most significant works of non-fiction to be published in recent times, bringing often overlooked perspectives and events to light with empathy. Praised by India's topmost scholars and critics, the book has already won various awards.

Ashutosh Bhardwaj is a bilingual fiction writer, literary critic, and is the only journalist in India to have won the prestigious Ramnath Goenka Award for Excellence in Journalism for four consecutive years. As a journalist, he has traveled across Central India and documented the conditions of tribes caught in the conflict between the Maoist insurgents and the police.

Publication: 4th **August 2022**

(Hardcover) ISBN: 978-1-910688-86-1

Cass J McMain

Rescuing Barbara

'Subdues one into complete and horrified fascination ...
The effects of a work like this linger for days' - *Karen Jennings (An Island)*

Ignoring her mother may have been a mistake.

During a bout of sobriety, Barbara implored her young daughter to turn her back on her if she began drinking again. Exhausted by her mother's alcoholism, Cass McMain finally took this advice and ignored everything the woman said or did for many years. She did not return calls, she did not visit, she did not react, send letters, or cajole. She simply turned away and waited for her mother to hit bottom or die trying. But as she discovered, bottom may be much farther down than one expects. Eventually, she is forced to wade in and untangle the mess her mother has created.

A gripping series of moments – painful, loving, desperate – *Rescuing Barbara* is a bitterly funny, and even lyrical true story about the inherent dangers of detachment ... and a reminder that predators are everywhere, waiting to fill in the gaps.

Publication: **2nd June 2022**

(Paperback) ISBN: 978-1-910688-40-3

Holland House Books

Holland House Books was founded in 2012 by Robert Peett. Its first novel, *The Absent Woman* by Marlene Lee, was published the following year. In 2021, Karen Jennings' novel *An Island* was longlisted for the Booker Prize.

Holland House Books specialises in literary fiction and non-fiction, crime fiction and poetry.. Notable titles include Nathalie Abi-Ezzi's *Paper Sparrows*, Emma Darwin's *This is Not a Book About Charles Darwin*, the story of a Holocaust survivor, *The Storyteller*, an extraordinary novel about mental illness, *Pax*, and the illustrated poem *Greta and the Labrador*.

Holland House Books' Novella Project, supported by the Arts Council, offers paid internships aimed at increasing diversity in writers and publishing professionals.

Robert Peett is a fellow of the Royal Society of Arts and gives masterclasses at Reading University and at other universities.